CASTLE CRAGS

CASTLE CRAGS

BUCK LYON

A Black Horse Western

ROBERT HALE · LONDON

DoN - 11/16 HoL.

ISBN 0 7090 4987 0

Robert Hale Limited
Clerkenwell House
Clerkenwell Green
London EC1R 0HT

Photoset in North Wales by
Derek Doyle & Associates, Mold, Clwyd.
Printed and bound in Great Britain by
WBC Bookbinders Ltd, Bridgend, Mid-Glamorgan.

ONE
An Encounter

There were broad valleys in the uplands country which appeared to be lost in the over-shadowing high peaks and granite slopes where junipers grew but where only an occasional spit of soft-woods, pine and fir, could survive.

The slopes had little soil, years of run-off had fairly well scoured down to bedrock. In ravines and gulches where earth settled, there was underbrush and pines at the lower elevations, fir trees higher up.

It was a spectacularly beautiful country, but few two-legged creatures had remained; beauty fed the soul but only deep soil fed the stomach. Here and there among those beautiful meadows with stirrup-high grass there were abandoned shacks; homesteaders, mostly from parts of the country where rich, deep soil made growing crops possible, learned the hard way what cattlemen could have told them: only seasonal grass flourished in shallow-dirt country.

Homesteaders rarely lasted long enough to 'prove up' on homesteaded land. What they had left behind, along with shattered dreams, were articles which had no place in shallow-earth country, ploughs, spike-toothed harrows, broken wagons, abandoned shacks which, after a few heavy winters, either collapsed or had roofs that sagged precariously.

It was high-country. The springs were sunbright and windy, the summers were something that left memories of glass-clear lakes, berry thickets so dense a man in armour could not have penetrated their thorny growth, and game in quantities no one had seen west of the Missouri River in a lifetime.

It was a quiet, ancient land. Horsemen riding across it felt as though they were the only humans on earth. Summer thunderstorms created noise, otherwise the bellow of bull elks in rutting season, the whining, snuffling sound of bear, the moonlight call of wolves, was the only noise.

Except at the lakes where trout jumping for May flies, splashed. There, once Indians had lived. All that was left now were the stone rings where hide tents had once been, and bones, occasionally broken spear points or arrowheads.

June was a good month to be in the Castle Crags country. The winds were only occasionally fitful, the nights were still cold, but the lengthening days were warm, as clear as still air made them.

A horseman camped on the south side of a large lake where fish practically jumped into his fry pan and days of brilliant sunshine, grass to his knees, a feeling of absolute isolation, made a high-country summer about as ideal as a man could hope for.

There was sign of cattle, usually dried to the consistency of ancient buffalo chips, mostly out in those emerald meadows. Infrequently he saw faint trails where cattle had come to drink at the lake, but he had crossed through a jagged tangle of mountains, riding a corkscrew route to reach the lake and its southward meadow without seeing anything but wildlife.

He had been two months on the trail, had stopped often so his buckskin horse could maintain its strength on graze and browse, had entered the mountains more miles north and easterly than he could calculate, and about the time he thought he would never break out of peaks and out-thrusts, granite, tallis and red cinnebar, he rode around a long bend following a wapiti trail, and there it was: The big grass meadow, the lake through a fringe of pines and firs, and after setting up camp and going exploring, the rotting-roofed massively built log house with the door lying on the ground, grass growing through its rotten wood, a pole corral long since decayed and fallen, and what remained of an old wagon, which was little more than the hardware.

After prowling the ruins he drew some conclusions. Whoever the settler had been, he had been a hard worker, talented at notching cabin logs, handy in most of the ways that a man had to be in unsettled country. But all the natural gifts on earth could not overcome thin soil and long, bitter winters. If men in this kind of country did not realise survival depended on living *with* nature, not trying to force nature to their will, their stay would inevitably be short.

The rusty old abandoned plough spoke eloquently of a homesteader's dream, and natural reality. This kind of country could not be ploughed.

The soil looked malleable, grass grew to stirrup-height, but the roots of seasonal graze only had to be a few inches deep. Below that a plough encountered either granite or hardpan.

The rider returned to his camp, shed everything but his long johns, his hat, boots and sidearm, fished, hunted when he felt a need for something beside fat trout, and loafed.

He was not a tall man, perhaps about average height. He was in his thirties, had taffy-coloured hair and green eyes. He also had the start of a multi-coloured beard. He had a razor, but it remained in the saddlebags hung overhead across a tree limb, where his booted saddlegun also hung.

He loafed, fished, hunted. lay in mid-day sunlight like a lizard, explored a little but not very extensively, and he thought about the back-breaking work that homesteader had done and the heart-breaking defeat he had succumbed to.

He also thought of other things, such as the reason he had entered those forbidding mountains which were west and south of Montana, where he had started from.

He knew something about heart-break.

He was lying on the riverbank in his red underwear, watching clouds pass, thinking back, remembering things so hard he did not hear the bear, not until he heard his hobbled horse hopping wildly. Then he raised up, twisted to look through trees out where the horse was in tall grass, and almost stopped breathing. The bear was a sow. She was big, scarred, old and seemed as stunned to see the man fifty feet ahead through the trees as he had been to see her.

It was springtime; the man thought of a cub. A sow bear with a cub was about as dangerous and deadly a critter as God had ever put on earth. They didn't wait when they saw what they considered an enemy, they snarled and came on like a freight train.

This old girl didn't move. She and the man in the red flannel underwear stared at each other for a long time. He scarcely breathed. His Winchester was back at camp, his sidearm also back there. Right at this moment he vividly recalled what an old man had once told him: 'Don't even go to bed without you got a gun close to hand.' If that old sow, he guessed her weight to be about four hundred pounds, had a cub, or even if she didn't have, the man had no escape. Climbing a tree, if he could reach one before she caught him, wouldn't help. She could climb better than he could. If he sprang up, ran out and dived into the lake, she could out-swim any man who'd ever been born.

He felt sweat running between his shoulder blades. He'd been a lot of places, had done a lot of things, and this was one hell of a place to get killed, where no one would even find his bones for maybe five, ten years.

The old sow was as pigeon-toed as all her kind were. She made one half-hearted paw to fling dirt with one front foot, which was ordinarily a warning, but she did not repeat it and she did not growl or raise her head to swing it from side to side and show her teeth, she just stood there looking at the man. Because bears had poor eyesight they normally reared up on their hind legs to test for scent. This old girl made no attempt to rear up, wag her head or show her teeth. She simply stood looking at the man in the red underwear.

He had every right to be scairt peeless, and he was, right up until the sow made a soft whining noise before she lumbered toward the lake, passed the man less than ten feet off, waddled to the water, ducked her head and drank, raised her head dripping water, looked over her shoulder at the man, then went back to drinking.

He considered running for all he was worth out across the meadow. He had encountered bear before, many times, he'd shot several who'd charged him, but the longer he watched this old girl, the more his bafflement increased.

When she had tanked up she turned, barely looked at the man and went bow-legging her way back through the trees, whining now and then as she cleared the timber and started in the direction of that dilapidated log house.

The man arose, got into the timber and watched. The old sow never deviated, she went directly over to that old log house and entered where the door had been.

The man waited but she did not emerge, so he went back, put on his britches, belted the sidearm into place and went looking for his horse.

Horses being constructed for flight, his buckskin wearing hobbles, was nowhere in sight on the meadow. He picked up the hop-tracks and walked more than a mile before he found the horse. It was standing like stone looking back toward the meadow. It paid no attention to the man who came up and caught it, but when he started to lead it back, it balked.

He had to see-saw to get it moving. He went around the meadow through the trees on the east side of the big clearing, and even then the horse spooked at everything, even birds in the trees.

Horses startled easily, but there were two varmints they panicked at just the scent: cougars and bears.

He remained with the horse until they were back at camp. The horse picked up bear-scent and set back, rolled its eyes and snorted. He left it tied to a tree, went over to start a cooking fire and looked back now and then. The horse was like a statue staring in the direction of that distant old log house. Bear scent was strong any time, as it was with most carrion eaters, but most carrion-eaters either had wings or were too small to cause much fear. His horse sweated without moving.

The man got his fire going, fried trout and missed the coffee he'd run out of two weeks back, and sat cross-legged to eat as he gazed in the direction of that distant house. He was irritated as much with the tomfool horse as he was at the old sow bear.

If this was her territory, and the way she acted it was, either the bear was going to have to leave or the man was.

But it puzzled him, the way she had acted. She evidently had no cub. She was old, which might have something to do with it, or she fought off rutting boar bears. For a fact she'd been in her share of battles. One ear was split in half, her snout had claw scars, her head and sides had missing hair.

The man ate, scoured his fry pan which served as a plate with grass, took the horse down to drink, which he did as fast as he could evidently expecting the bear to come charging and bellowing at any moment. The man was disgusted.

'You damned idiot, she's over yonder in the house. If she'd wanted horse meat, partner, she could have caught you. Even with hobbles in open country she most likely could have caught you ... Except maybe not, she's old.'

The horse had distended nostrils and rolling eyes when it faced around with water dripping. It and the man had been partnering for three years. They got along well. This was the first time the man had ever seen the buckskin so terrified.

It was also the first time they had encountered a bear at close range. The man tied the horse again, stood gazing in the direction of the old log house, and swore under his breath. He was not going to walk over to try and run that old sow off, because the next time they met she might not act as she had before. He also had no desire to go inside, or even very close outside, to try and roust the old girl to run her into the hills with a couple of pistol shots.

One thing was a cinch, tonight he was not going to get much sleep, and tomorrow if the old girl decided to drink again before she went back to her hunting ground, he was going to have to do something. He did not want to shoot her, partly because he had nothing against bears, partly because when she could have killed him, she hadn't, she had acted as though the world was large enough for them both.

He sat in the dusk watching to see if she would leave the log house. He had never encountered a bear like that old sow before.

He was more interested than curious. It occurred to him as dusk was settling, that this was not only her lake, but the meadow was also her territory and that log house served as her den.

If any of this was true, it was truly remarkable that she hadn't at least mauled him, slapped him around. Bears were very territorial animals.

It wouldn't hurt the horse to go all night without feed, horses normally did not graze at night. The man settled his coiled shellbelt beside his blanket roll, holster-up within a foot of his head, shed his britches, boots and hat, lay back gazing at a million pinpricks of light as dusk turned to full night, and for the first time in a while, his thoughts were on the present not the past.

There was something un-natural about that old sow. He could not put his finger on it, but when they had been staring at each other she had not looked anything other than surprised; she had not looked frightened nor belligerent, she had simply stood there gazing at him. She had walked past to drink and hadn't looked back at him until she was ready to depart.

If he ever told anyone of this encounter they would not believe him. It was common knowledge that when anything, two-legged or four-legged, invaded bear territory, they would either be run off or killed.

He heard the horse snort and sat up reaching for his sixgun. Nothing was moving on the meadow that he could see. His horse was standing head-up little ears pointing, staring in the direction of the log house.

The man swore, pulled on his boots, his britches, took the gun and went scouting boldly across the open meadow where a sickle moon cast barely enough light to see by.

He was within a dozen yards of the log house when he heard a sound he had heard many times before; a bear was pushing its way through underbrush and trees up the westerly slope behind the log house.

He stood in puny moonlight for a long time listening. She was going up that rugged, partly timbered slope without stopping.

The man spat, shoved the sixgun into the waistband of his trousers and turned back, satisfied the old girl had left the immediate area, probably in order to be on her hunting ground when daylight arrived.

The man returned to his camp, shed attire, climbed back into his blankets with the gun close, and swore to himself.

Tonight he'd be able to sleep. His horse wouldn't as long as the old sow's scent was in the air, but by daylight that should be gone, so he could hobble the buckskin in tall grass again.

But if this was indeed her territory, she would be back. The man groaned about that. One of them, the old sow or the man and his buckskin horse would have to leave.

TWO
A Cloud over Paradise

Morning arrived with dazzling brilliance but no particular warmth until about ten o'clock. The man was good at estimating time. He hadn't owned a time-piece in years. In his way of life only dawn and dark were relevant. As for mealtime, his stomach told him all he had to know about that.

He crossed over to the old log house, scouted it carefully, saw tracks in drying dew where the old girl had departed in the night or early morning, followed them into a timbered swale and turned back. The old sow probably were not in that timber but he had no intention of going in there to find out.

By the time he had finished breakfast, had hobbled his horse in tall grass on the east side of the big meadow where it could not pick up bear-scent, there was heat in the new day.

He went down to the lake to fish, this time wearing both his britches and his belt-gun. He intended to take an all-over bath later on.

Because the old sow had loomed large in his immediate surroundings, he thought about her off and on while fishing. Once, the buckskin horse had thrown up its head and whinnied. He went back

15

through the trees, saw nothing, the horse was back eating, so he went back to clean his trout before taking them to camp, and tested the water. The sun was high, the morning was warm but the water was colder than a banker's heart.

He covered the fish with wet leaves, put them where direct sunlight could not reach, put on his hat and hiked around the east side of the lake. He found several ancient stone rings, in one place a collapsed burial platform with the mummy-bundle pretty well eaten through by varmints, and stopped in that place because there was a slight out-thrust of land where fish were jumping.

He could look back, see his camp, the spit of trees behind it, and some of the big meadow. He could not see his horse, but horses were liable to hunt shade when all the pleats were out of their stomachs.

He sat on a big rock half in shade, half in sunshine, watching trout jump, ranging an appreciative look across the lake and along its timbered shoreline.

An eagle soared into view, so high the rings on his outstretched wings were not visible. The man shoved his hat back, watched the bird for a while, then started back.

This, he told himself was what God had made man for – or someone had anyway – and this was probably how He – or someone – had intended men to live, strong enough to protect themselves but in such surroundings enjoying a depth of peacefulness found in no other setting.

As a stockman he felt reasonably certain that soon now, with warm weather, good feed, abundant shade and water, someone would probably drift cattle into the high country. He'd ridden for outfits that followed this natural cycle; this was the kind of country they used for summer grazing.

He had seen sign of cattle since his first day on the meadow.

He abruptly thought of the old sow: stockmen killed bear on sight. How had that old girl managed to stay alive as long as she obviously had?

There was no way to make excuses; bears were meat-eaters. Cows heavy with calf would have their babies in country like this at this time of year. Baby calves would be helpless against that old sow.

Well, as he hunkered to fry some fish, everywhere a man went he ran into what seemed to be contradictions, until he'd been around long enough to understand how, and why, things worked.

But he knew for a fact that any stockman who ran onto that old sow, would kill her out of hand. He'd seen it done with both bear and cougar a hundred times.

When he finished his meal with the sun high, he cleaned up, tossed aside his hat, removed the belt-gun and its shellbelt, stretched out for a nap, and forgot about not seeing the buckskin.

Later, with the sun bearing away toward distant rims, he went down to the lake for his bath. The water was still cold enough to freeze the *pelotes* on a brass monkey, but his reward was to sit on a rock in the altogether to let sunshine dry and warm him.

It was while he was perched there that he heard the buckskin whinny for the second time today. He turned to arise – and froze.

A rider was sitting a sorrel horse back at his camp as still as stone, watching him. Except for one thing he wouldn't have been too worried, although he hadn't heard the rider pass from the meadow through the trees.

It was a woman.

She was riding astride with a buckskin split skirt. Her shirt was flannel, well-worn as were the roping gloves on her hands.

He made a sickly smile sitting twisted. She reined around and remained with her back to him for as long as was required for him to get his britches and boots, drop the old hat atop his head and say, 'I'm decent, ma'am.'

She reined back around. She was handsome in an outdoors sort of way. He guessed her to be a little shy of his own age. She had dark hair and pale blue eyes. She looped both reins, removed the gloves and finally spoke.

'That's a nice buckskin you have.'

He replied as she probably expected him to. 'Yes'm. We been partners a long time.' Then he thought of the old sow. 'Yesterday a sow bear came along and liked to scairt the whey out of him.'

Her expression was gravely expressionless, but her eyes crinkled slightly at what he had said. 'Old, scarred snout, one split ear?'

'That's her.'

The woman finally swung to the ground as she said, 'That'd be Molly. I raised her from an orphan cub.'

That clarified the mystery of the bear, 'I thought there was something different about her. She came through those trees behind you an' when I looked up there she was.'

The handsome woman almost smiled; she could imagine how the man must have felt. 'She's a pet. But she's still a bear.'

The man sighed. 'I guess this is her territory. She spent last night in that old log house over yonder.'

The woman stood at the head of horse with one rein in her hand. 'That's where I was born. My father found her half starved in the timber and brought her home. I was about ten years old. We grew up together. She didn't have a mother and I didn't have a playmate. We even hunted together.'

'Good thing no stockman saw her on that meadow.'

'Every summer I get the riders together and explain about Molly. If one of them shoots her he'll answer to me … I'm Evelyn Scott.'

The man accepted that. 'I'm John Lane.'

'Mister Lane, how far north of the lake have you ridden?'

'I settled in, haven't explored much except for that log house and maybe quarter way around the lake on the east side.'

Evelyn Scott raised an arm. 'Do you see that high peak, higher than the others around it, the peak with snow on it year round?'

He looked. He had admired that upthrust. 'Yes'm. Pretty hard country I'd guess.'

She dropped her arm. 'Not hard at all unless you stay in the mountains. My home place is just below that peak about three miles from here. If you'd gone up around the north end of the lake you'd have seen the buildings.' She waited a moment then spoke again. 'This is Tandy Meadow. My parents home-steaded here twenty-five years ago. My mother is buried here. Up that gulch behind the log house.' She paused again before speaking in that same almost inflectionless, matter-of-fact way.

'I was surprised to find you here. It's time to bring in the cattle so I rode ahead to see how the feed was. Mister Lane, how long do you expect to camp here?'

John Lane had done some calculating. If she had

been born here to some folks named Tandy, and had introduced herself as Evelyn Scott, she had married someone who owned land and cattle in this high country.

'I hadn't thought much about it, Missus Scott. I just sort of came out of those northwesterly mountains – and there it was – as peaceful and pretty a spot as I've seen ... But I expect if you folks are goin' to drift cattle in, it'd be better if I wasn't here, wouldn't it?'

She did not reply immediately, she instead gazed out where only a few trout were still jumping. This time of day although May flies still circled and dipped a foot or so above the lake, trout had gone deeper to avoid the warming surface water.

When she replied her tone was different, slightly subdued. 'It'll be about two weeks before the marking is finished. We won't drive for a week after that.'

She returned her gaze to him and without a hint of a smile, said, 'I've got a cake of soap in my saddlebags.'

She turned to dig it out. She didn't hand it to him, she put it on a rock, swung into the saddle, nodded and rode away.

John Lane would have been red-faced if she hadn't so abruptly departed. He went back to the rock beside the lake and sat in sunshine. Well, that explained about the old sow, and it also broadened his knowledge of his surroundings, but what kept him pondering the most was the way the handsome woman had never raised her voice, never said anything not immediately relevant to their meeting, and seemed not to know how to smile.

She wasn't beautiful, she wasn't even exactly pretty. She was handsome, sturdily put together, the kind of a woman who seemed entirely at ease in the company

of strangers, the kind of woman who left a man half
put-off, half admiring.

He went out to visit the buckskin horse. It was
dozing hipshot in the shade of a huge pine tree,
opened one eye, then closed it again. Its lower lip was
hanging, When an occasional insect came along, it
lazily wagged its tail.

The horse was content, which was probably the
only human feeling horses shared with people, except
for fear and hunger.

John Lane had not thought about moving on. In
fact, with all summer ahead and with no responsibi-
lities behind, he would have been perfectly content to
remain on – Tandy – meadow until autumn.

When he returned to camp the sun was low, there
were shadows on the off-side of big trees, the lake was
a flat turquoise surface reflecting green from its
shores and blue from the flawless heavens.

At dusk with fish frying, he heard his horse again,
went through the trees and saw why. The old sow was
shambling in his direction across the meadow. She
ignored the frightened horse and he, for his own
reasons, still acted frightened half to death, but the
man who knew him best, recognised less terror than
before.

Maybe, over the next week or so, the buckskin
would develop a kind of very leary tolerance of the
bear. But it would never go beyond that.

The man shoved more twigs under his fry pan and
put in three more trout. As an experiment. He did
not look up from cooking even when he heard the old
sow whiningly complaining as she approached, which
was as natural to bear as talking was to men.

He put the cooked fish aside to cool before arising
to watch the sow come back exactly as she had the day

before, and stop, wrinkling her nose and solemnly regarding the two-legged creature.

As before, they went through their ritual of watching one another for several minutes before the sow ambled past to drink. The man waited until she was finished and was returning, then crossed her path, put a cooked fish on a rock, went back and watched.

The sow sniffed, halted to trace out the scent, went over and ate the fish. The man laughed. She turned to solemnly regard him. He said, 'Molly?' and threw another fish.

She ate that one too, and waited. He tossed her the last fish, which she scarfed down like a dog, without seeming to chew or be bothered by bones.

They looked at one another until she decided there would be no more fish, then went on her way across the meadow and into the old log house.

John Lane leaned on a tree until she was out of sight, then shook his head, went back to clean up after their meal, and smile to himself imagining the look on Evelyn Scott's mother's face when her father had brought home the little cub.

Bears weren't made to be pets, although sow bears had been tamed, but if it had been a boar bear …

John returned to the rock by the lake. Good thing he hadn't been warming his front when she rode up. He turned scarlet, skipped a rock across the still water and ruefully smiled. It must have shocked the hell out of her, a naked man being where she hadn't expected even one with clothes on.

He bedded down wondering where he and buckskin would go now. He knew landforms only in the vaguest way, and for a fact he did not want to ride into any towns nor for that matter, hang his saddle where there were people.

Due west somewhere the mountains ended. They always ended, somewhere. He had an idea he was in Oregon but wouldn't have bet a plugged dollar on that.

Nor did it matter, what mattered was that new country held his interest, new scenes, new views, new kinds of flowers, birds and even new bears.

He laughed aloud.

A sow bear as large as any he'd ever seen, shinnying up to a stranger would have scairt anyone out of their wits, but Molly had not acted quite right from the beginning.

How lonesome a little girl had to have been up in this uninhabited high country to adopt a cub bear as her friend.

He went to sleep wondering about that un-smiling woman who talked like a man and who evidently also thought like one. Except for obvious differences, a man would have to be awful darned lonely to be interested in this woman, handsome or not.

In the morning he eyed the bar of soap she'd left on the rock, shrugged, took it down to the water's edge and lathered himself so well he thought he might as well shave, which he did, dulling a perfectly good straight razor in the process.

There was something else. When he was through washing and shaving he smelled like ten nights in a Turkish harem.

Evidently Mister Scott's woman only used store-bought soap. He'd used it too, once or twice before, but the smell of lilacs which he liked on a bush, he did not like on his face. Soap, the kind he'd used most of his life came in tan chunks, was odourless and sometimes a little grainy, but soap was unimportant beyond its basic, sole, purpose.

He returned to camp with the towel over one shoulder, put on his shirt and turned his head from one side to the other. Each time that fragrance reached his nostrils.

He fried more trout, stoked the fire a little and because he felt eyes on his back he looked around. The old sow was standing there about fifteen feet away wrinkling her nose. Bear could wrinkle their noses more than any animal that lived in the mountains. Old Molly was practically twisting her nose off her face. The man laughed, tossed her a fish from the fry pan, which she sniffed, pawed at but would not eat until it cooled.

The man thought it had been a mistake to feed her last night, but he had and now there was no way to un-do it. He had a hunch that for the next week or so that he was in camp near the lake, he was going to have to catch twice as many fish as he normally caught.

He fed the sow all his cooked fish. She stood waiting. He spoke to her as though she understood. 'I only got enough left to feed myself. Come back after sundown, I'll have more.'

The old sow turned and walked back through the trees as though she had understood every word. John Lane stood up to watch as she bypassed the log house and went up the far slope where he lost sight of her among the trees.

It was a little eerie. No one would ever believe what he could tell them. He knew better than to ever mention this bizarre acquaintanceship in a bunkhouse or around a roundup fire.

It had been a little over a week since the last night-frost, and perhaps if he hadn't shaved he wouldn't have noticed it so quickly, but now there were mosquitoes.

The blood-sucking little pests kept to the shade during daylight, and the man's camp was also in the shade.

He put green bows on his fire, which did a fair job of getting rid of the creatures, but a man would have to spend half a day gathering enough green limbs to get any rest.

He walked down to tell the buckskin horse their idyllic life was about to end. The horse, accustomed to being talked to, looked at the man with more than lack of comprehension, like every animal who did as well and usually better in the wild than it did in captivity, to the buckskin horse John Lane who had always treated him well, was a friend, one he could just as well have done without.

He looked and listened, then turned his ample rump toward the two-legged thing and went back to grazing.

THREE
A Decision

The handsome woman had said they'd be working cattle for the next two weeks, which meant her husband had a lot of cattle. It also meant John Lane did not have to hasten plans for departure.

The week after the cattle had been worked it was common among some stockmen to keep them close so riders could watch for infection, screw worms, or whatnot before driving them to distant upland ranges where they'd spend the summer.

John Lane continued his comfortable existence, fishing, resting, feeding Molly who had become as much a fixture at camp as the trees.

He learned something about bears from the old sow. She could be relied upon to show up for breakfast and supper exactly when the lowering sun was at a particular place among the treetops. He also learned that as frightening as any four hundred pound four-legged critter with big sharp teeth and little tan eyes could be, Molly liked to be scratched and have ticks picked off her.

It took several days of caution before the man touched the old girl, but for her part anyone who fed her was also required to scratch her. She would walk right up to the man, lean until they touched and raise her snout turning it slightly from side to side, which meant scratching.

He scratched, he fed her, he even talked to her, and maybe the handsome woman played with her, but damned if he was going to.

The more he was around Molly the more he wondered about a number of things which he thought he would never have answers to, but that was an incorrect surmise.

The woman re-appeared at the lake four days after her first visit. This time her hair was held in back by a red ribbon and she wore a heavy white shirt, but the roping gloves, the split buckskin skirt and the expression were the same, except when she saw the old sow and swung to the ground ignoring the man to go over and scratch as she said. 'Not much longer, Molly.'

John Lane said, 'Good morning, ma'm.'

She replied without looking around. 'Good morning, Mister Lane … Has Molly moved in with you?'

He smiled and sank down on a punky ancient deadfall fir watching the woman and the sow bear. 'No one's ever going to believe this, a sow bear coming up wanting to be scratched.'

She turned, went to the same deadfall he was sitting on and sat. Molly lingered, but only briefly. As she went shambling in the direction of the log house Evelyn Scott watched and said, 'That's home to her. She slept next to the stove until she got too big. My mother wasn't fond of a bear in the house, but Molly thought she was a person. Still, my mother put her out as soon as her second summer came round.'

The woman turned. 'You're a rangeman, Mister Lane?'

'Yes'm, except that this year I'm foot loose.'

'Did you ever rangeboss?'

John Lane hesitated before answering. 'For three years, mostly I just rode.'

The handsome woman studied her boots as she spoke again. 'This is isolated country, Mister Lane. The nearest town is thirty miles southeast. Berksville.' She lapsed into silence before speaking again. 'Hiring riders each spring isn't hard. Keeping them is.' She looked up at him, grave and unsmiling. 'Rangemen like their Saturday nights in town.'

He partially agreed. 'Some do. It's good to break the work once in a while.'

She went back to studying her boots. 'I've never hired anyone I've found in the uplands.'

He watched her profile with dawning thoughts.

'I suppose because over the last twenty years I've only met five, maybe six riders up in here. They were moving through.'

He thought this could drag on for an hour so he said, 'Missus Scott, I get the feelin' you're leading up to something.'

She continued to look at her boots, with a very faint lift to the outer edges of her lips. 'I need a rangeboss, Mister Lane.' She finally faced him, pale eyes stone-steady.

He made a soundless small sigh. 'They're around, ma'm. Especially this time of year.'

She did not dispute this but went back to what she'd said before. 'I know that. But like I said, thirty miles is too far to ride for a break on Saturday night.'

Now he was sure his hunch had been correct, and again he took the bull by the horns. 'Missus Scott, I know it's none of my business, but your husband ....'

'Is dead, Mister Lane. He died four years ago. A horse fell on him coming out of the mountains.'

His gaze left the pale eyes and returned. 'I'm sorry.'

'Mister Lane, a man who's camped up here, likes the area, and isn't working ... Someone who has been a foreman ...'

It was his turn to look away. He gazed through the trees in the direction of the old log house. Molly was nowhere in sight. He thought she had probably gone up to her hunting ground.

The handsome woman waited. When he said nothing she spoke again. 'I'll turn it back on you, Mister Lane. It's none of my business but do you have some reason for being up here, not working in riding season, staying apart?'

He brought his gaze back to her. 'About that soap,' he said, and she suddenly laughed. It was an almost musical sound. He stared until she said, 'I can smell lilac over here.'

He scratched his jaw. Her laughter had startled him, had scattered his thoughts. He would have bet new money she didn't know how to laugh.

He pondered a moment then told her a story. 'I was married up north. I rangebossed for her paw. He was a good man in his way, but we jangled each other. For three years. Then my wife died ... I left, just saddled up Buck and kept riding.'

'How long ago did she die, Mister Lane?'

'Last summer.'

The handsome woman went back to studying her boots. Nothing was said between them for a long time. The buckskin horse was warily approaching the camp, head up, eyes rolling. It was the closest place he could get water, but it was obvious with every step he was prepared to whirl and hop for his life.

The woman softly said, 'It takes time, Mister Lane. A long time. I had the ranch to run. I kept busy. But at night I'd remember.' She looked out where the buckskin was making his mincing approach to the trees. She watched him too, until he spoke again.

'I know. That's why I rode so far, looked at new country, different critters, higher mountains – and this meadow beside the lake.'

He forced a smile at her. 'I lived off the country as I went along, skirted towns, even little settlements, and ran out of coffee an' salt and directly now I've got to get my horse re-shod, maybe down at the town you named a while back.'

'Berksville ... Do you know how to shoe, Mister Lane?'

'Yes'm, I've done my share.'

'There is a smithy at the ranch. It's only about three miles. That's a lot closer than Berkville.'

He asked what had happened to her last foreman. She replied with resignation in her voice. 'We were too far from everywhere. And I don't think he liked working for a woman. He never said so, but there were little things, remarks to the riders ... He'd been with my husband seven years. He was a good stockman, Mister Lane, but one day this spring he upped and quit. Drew his time and rode off. He said he needed to get away from mountains for a while. That left two riders and me. They're older men. They've been on the ranch for years.'

'How many cattle, ma'm?'

'Six hundred cows, forty cows to a bull. Last year's big steers ready to go south to the railroad pens this fall. I'll cull heifers in the fall too, keep back replacements and send the others on the drive' ... Mister Lane?'

When he turned their eyes met and held. 'Yes'm?'

'If it doesn't work out, I'll understand.'

This conversation, the personal parts of it anyway, had troubled his emotions. The longer they looked at one another the more drawn to her he was. 'Maybe if I had a day or two ... I'll ride to your place no later than day after tomorrow, if that's all right ... And whether it works out or not, my name is John.'

She almost smiled as she arose from the old log. She turned and offered her hand. They shook like two men, she went over, mounted her horse, nodded at him and rode away back through the trees.

He sank back down on the deadfall. His horse had tanked up at the lakeshore and was now standing with his back to the water looking warily in all directions. The man laughed. 'She's miles from here by now ... Let me tell you somethin' partner, don't go by smell so much. Right now I don't smell like anyone who ever rode you.'

He waited until the horse had gone back through the trees and was grazing in hot sunlight before walking down to the lake to sit on the big rock.

They had something in common after all. The first time they met she hadn't made a very good impression. He still wondered about her, but after their talk, he wondered less and understood more.

He looked to the future. Trailing cattle out of the high country to Berksville, or wherever the railroad corrals were, would use up a lot of time next autumn. But he'd done that many times.

Working for a woman – well – he'd heard bunkhouse talk about that, but he had no feelings about working for a woman one way or the other.

His summation was about as they had said sitting on the log. If it didn't work out, he'd ride on.

He got his fishing gear, hiked part way around where that old Indian camp had been and caught dinner for himself and for the sow bear in about an hour, gutted the fish where he caught them, returned to camp and rolled the carcasses in wet leaves in the shade, then did something he hadn't done much lately, he rolled and lighted a smoke.

Fate was a real puzzler at times. But it really hadn't been an urge to explore that had kept him riding, it had been the distractions which kept his mind off something painful. The question he had to decide was whether being in one place for any length of time would work as well as changing views in different country, being alone, remembering tender things that did not hurt, as much as the sense of loss. Keeping his mind occupied with new sights, new encounters.

His reverie was interrupted by loud snorts from the buckskin. He returned to camp without even looking out there, got a fire going and started frying trout. Molly's grumbling was audible before she was visible. He shook his head. Distractions? Hell no one would ever believe John Lane, tophand, was keeping company in a highland meadow with an old sow bear named Molly, who had been around people so much she thought she was one.

When he turned the sow was sitting on her haunches like a dog wrinkling her nose and waiting. He laughed at her. She dropped down on all fours and shambled over to within a few feet of him, eyes fixed on the skillet. He knew he could have reached over and scratched her, but a lifelong wariness around bears inhibited him. But he talked to her, explained that the fish were not ready yet, told her constantly wiggling and wrinkling her nose and slobbering was not going to make them cook any faster.

He also told her something else. 'Your boss sort of grows on a man, did you know that, old girl? She's ... I can't put my finger on it. She's a fine lookin' woman – not pretty like dancehall girls I've seen. An' she don't seem to want to laugh or smile. Molly, what d'you think?'

The sow's patience had a limit. She raised a clawed large paw toward the skillet, heat made her pull back quickly. She licked the paw then, without any warning, licked the man's cheek.

He leaned away, wiped his face on a sleeve and told her to mind her damned manners, and whatever she'd been eating made her breath smell terrible.

Molly fidgeted and slobbered more. The man finally gave up, what the hell, bears ate raw fish so half-cooked fish shouldn't be objectionable. He tipped the skillet, trout slid to the ground, but Molly knew about hot things, she pawed carefully, but made no move to eat the fish until they had cooled. This allowed John Lane time to prepare his own supper. The trouble was that when he ate, he chewed, when Molly was finally able to eat her fish she did away with the lot in three or four mouthfuls and did not seem to chew at all. She watched the man eat, and whined.

He gave up in disgust, gave her three of his five trout and ate as fast as he could so they would finish about the same time.

Molly watched the man cover his fire with dirt, pull grass to scour his fry pan, turned and waddled back through the trees in the direction of the log house. The man grinned, a bear's tail was little better than no tail at all. Molly waddled on course, did not once look over where the bug-eyed horse was staring, not moving but clearly prepared to.

The man finished his chores, went down to the lake

to watch the sun set. In the morning he would ride north in the direction of that mighty peak that resembled a castle. Not to see the woman, to see her ranch. A man should reconnoitre before he hired on.

He bedded down with dusk on the way, listened to coyotes in the distance making one of their coursing runs in a strong pack, paid no heed and supposed his horse wouldn't either.

There was one benefit of having Molly around. Her scent would keep coyotes, wolves, just about anything away except perhaps another bear.

He had an errant thought; bears, even baby ones, were liable to eat anything they could kill – they also ate things other animals had killed and had abandoned. Even young bears just naturally ate carrion. Evelyn Scott's mother must have had the patience of a saint. A carrion-eating bear in a house no larger than the log house was, especially during winter when windows and doors were kept closed while the stove smouldered, would have made the house smell almost sickeningly bad.

He was curious about the handsome woman's parents. Her father in particular. The longer he had these thoughts before going to sleep, the more he was subconsciously deciding he would work for her.

In the morning he arose ahead of daylight and fished until it was light. He had the fire going, the trout cooking half an hour before Molly came grumbling, growling, whining through the trees.

This time he was ready. Molly did not seem surprised or pleased that her breakfast was ready when she came out of the trees. She ate, turned without so much as a grunt of gratitude and went hiking in the direction of her hunting area.

The man watched, shook his head and told himself

that even if the handsome woman had not appeared to invite him off her meadow, he would have had to leave anyway, unless he wanted to spend the rest of the summer making sure that old sow was fed amply and on time.

He felt an odd fondness for that four hundred pounds of lethal violence which did not square with everything he had been told as a youngster as well as what he had heard later; bears were as deadly and as dangerous as anything alive, and while they looked clumsy and smelled terrible, they could out-run any man alive and a lot of fairly fast horses.

They were, he had heard a hundred times, unpredictable as the weather. Molly was old. He calculated her age from her worn teeth and the age of the handsome woman, to be somewhere between sixteen and maybe twenty-five. She did not show any of the rheumatism bears evinced as they got older, and the man never doubted that in a fight she could still roust mating boar bears that came snuffling around.

He cleaned up the camp, brought the buckskin horse in to be rigged out, and had to let the billet out two notches and he still had little slack in the *latigo*. The buckskin horse had also fared very well up here. Too well; a short run or a long lope would have him dripping water in rivulets. That was one thing about green feed and horses; it came as close to foundering them if they were left hock deep in it very long as anything else.

As he rode away from the camp he let the horse pick the gait. They had to circle half around the west side of the lake before the man saw shod horse track left by the woman.

He wasn't going to have to hunt for the ranch, all

he had to do was follow the shod-horse tracks, they followed a well-worn trail.

He rode through big timber much of the way so there was no appreciable warmth for an hour or so, not until he came out on a promontory where the trail sashayed around on the downward side toward a picture-postcard setting.

The meadow was larger than the one he had left, the buildings were log with sugar pine shakes on the roof. There was the usual scattering of out-buildings and a large barn.

There were fruit trees, which indicated a female hand, the corrals were round and in good repair. He sat a while, long enough to smoke, before edging the buckskin down the trail toward the yard.

The monolithic peak called Castle Crag rose almost directly behind the yard. It was toweringly high and intimidating to someone who had never seen it up close before.

The setting was magnificent; this was late spring, anyone with half an eye could tell that in winter this place would have more than enough snow to keep folks cabin-bound for several months.

She had been right; it *was* isolated.

FOUR
Visitors

He hailed the yard from a hundred yards out. The only response he got was a booming bark from a very large, shaggy dog with sagging jowls and a big head. He barked and wagged his tail at the same time. The man decided to take a chance and trust in the rear end instead of the barking end.

He tied up in front of the barn the huge dog walked over to be scratched. John Lane told him that as a protector he was a dismal failure, but as a barking critter, from a distance he would scare off just about anything.

They went to look in the barn. It was empty. They went to crack the door of the bunkhouse. It also was empty. The dog conveyed him to the main-house and waited until knocking brought no response, then went with the man back to the horse, led them to the shoeing shed, and sank down comfortably in dust as the man shed his shirt, hat, beltgun, dumped the saddle, cross-tied the horse and went to work.

The forge had a good bellows, the rest of it had been handmade of mortised stone. It was old, every usable kind of blacksmithing tool was there. In fact the yard with huge old trees, the buildings, even the

37

rocked-up springhouse was old.

The man had to assume that this ranch had not been founded by the handsome woman's husband, it had more than likely been founded by his father.

He fired things up, pumped the bellows a few times to keep coals hot, then went to work pulling shoes and making four new ones. It was a time-consuming chore but the day was warm without being hot, which made forge and anvil work less of a chore.

The dog slept, no amount of shaping steel over the anvil induced him to even raise an eyelid. The dog, the entire place, even its timeless setting, was serenely quiet.

There were horses in the middle distance grazing slowly. John Lane worked for the better part of two hours, was clinching and rasping the final off-side rear hoof when he saw the big dog raise its head looking northwesterly. He paused to mop sweat, looked, saw nothing and hoisted the hoof for the last few licks with the rasp.

The dog got up, stood stiff but made no sound although something clearly had his full attention. John Lane led his horse across to the barn, stalled and hayed it, found a stone trough out back, leaned to wash in water cold enough to waken the dead, and was straightening up to dry off when a man spoke quietly from the rear barn opening.

'Mister Barnes?'

John Lane turned. There were three of them, unsmiling hard, grizzled individuals, staring at him. He finished drying and said. 'John Lane.'

The speaker's droopy moustache made him appear either inherently gloomy, or solemn. 'Can you prove it?' he asked.

Lane had left his shellbelt and sidearm hanging on

a peg at the smithy. The three strangers were armed. 'Well, I don't have my name on my saddle, if that's what you mean ... Who are you?'

A heretofore tall man with narrowed eyes said, 'Just answer the questions. Can you prove you're not Arthur Barnes?'

'Mister, I can't prove I'm not Abraham Lincoln.'

'How many riders up here, Mister Lane?'

'Two and the lady who owns the place. There don't seem to be anyone around. I rode in this morning, didn't find a soul.'

'Did you make that fire in the smithy?'

'Yes. I shod my horse over there. He's the buckskin in the stall behind you.'

'Well now,' asked the tall man, 'You don't just ride into someone's yard and make yourself shoes an' use their tools an' all without their permission, do you?'

John Lane eased down on the stone trough. They were not openly hostile but they were close to it. He asked who they were. The answer he got was another question.

'You got some idea where the lady an' her riders might be?'

He considered the cold-eyed tall man. They had ignored his question so he ignored their question. 'If you want to settle in I expect the lady an' her two riders will be along directly.' He arose to cross back through the barn toward the smithy. The man who so far had not said a word blocked the way. He was about John Lane's height and heft, maybe a tad younger. He didn't say a word, he just blocked the way until one of the other men spoke behind Lane. 'Mister, you don't fit the description, but descriptions been wrong before. We come a hell of a distance to talk to Mister Barnes. I expect we'll do what you said settle in an' wait – but you're not goin' over where you left your gun hangin' on a peg. We'll just sort of wait together.'

John turned slowly. The speaker gave him look for look. From what this man had just said they had evidently scouted up the yard, had watched him leave the gun and lead his horse over to be stalled, and what that meant to John Lane, was that whoever Arthur Barnes was, if he worked for Evelyn Scott, when he returned from a day's work he was going to get one hell of a surprise.

The stocky man blocking the way made a sour remark while Lane's back was to him. He said, 'Everett, this is Barnes as sure as I'm standin' here.'

The narrowed-eyed man with the droopy moustache replied quietly, which seemed to be his natural way of speaking. 'The age is wrong, Billy. Maybe the description is wrong in other ways, maybe not, but the age sure as hell is. This feller's no older'n you are.'

Billy thought he had the solution. 'I can find out who he is, age or no age.'

John Lane faced back around slowly. Billy was ready, his eyes were fiery. Without a word John Lane struck from the belt. Billy went over backwards, his hat rolled and he did not move. Two guns were cocked behind Lane. He faced the other men. 'I told you I'm not named Barnes, I never met a man named Barnes in this country. If you fellers got a quarrel with Barnes you'd ought to make sure you got him before you get rough.'

The man named Everett, eased down the dog, leathered his sixgun and looked at the taller man. 'Jeff ...?'

'I got a feelin' you're right, Everett. This ain't Arthur Barnes. But if Barnes is out with the woman an' another rider, we can't have this feller warning them.'

Everett went over to hoist Billy to his feet. He had a purpling swelling alongside his jaw on the left side and Everett had to steady him or he'd have fallen.

Everett looked at John Lane. 'He was just doin' what he figured was right.'

John Lane said, 'So was I, mister ... You got a name?'

'Everett Holt. ... Deputy United States Marshal.'

John Lane let his breath out slowly, looked back at the tall man named Jeff, and looked for something to sit on.

Billy recovered slowly, his jaw hurt, there was a flung-back trickle of blood from one corner of his mouth. He eyed Lane a moment then also sought something to sit on. The three strangers now knew one thing, whoever the man was they had thought might be Arthur Barnes, could hit like the kick of an army mule.

Everett sent the man called Jeff to fetch their horses to be stalled in the barn. Billy went out back to the trough. He and Everett could hear him splashing in cold water.

Everett sat down and pointed across the barn as he said, 'Set. Just set there an' be quiet.'

John Lane obeyed. 'Who is Arthur Barnes?' he asked.

The federal lawman gazed around the barn before answering in that quiet voice. 'I'm interested in how you come to be on the Scott place.'

John Lane put a whimsical gaze upon the other man. 'You tell me who Arthur Barnes is an' I'll tell you how I come to be here.'

Marshal Holt replied quietly. 'It's a long story an' it

goes back a number of years. Arthur Barnes an'
another feller stopped two coaches, one with mail, the
other carryin' a strongbox of new money from the
Denver mint. Barnes shot the gunguard. There's a
federal law about somethin' like that; the gunguard
he killed was a federal messenger.'

John Lane considered what he had been told
before asking his next question. 'How long ago,
Marshal?'

'Six, seven years back.' Holt looked steadily across
the barn runway. 'The gov'ment takes a real mean
look at shootin' federal men. We never give up,
Mister Lane. Never.'

John settled his back against the front of the stall
holding his buckskin horse. Billy returned with the
cobwebs gone, leaned on a barn upright and
regarded John Lane from an expressionless face.

Jeff returned leading three saddled horses with
blanket rolls behind each cantle and booted
saddleguns slung butts forward under each saddle
fender. Without a word he off-saddled the animals,
turned them into stalls and looked for a fork to pitch
them feed with. The forks, like the hay, were
overhead in a huge maw. Access was by way of a tree
trunk with slats nailed across it.

Billy worked his jaw. There was nothing broken but
pain made him desist. He went out back and did not
return. The tall man was climbing down after forking
feed to the stalled animals, when Everett Holt asked a
question of the man sitting opposite him.

'All right, mister: Now you tell me how you come to
be here ... This ain't exactly an easy place to find.'

John Lane told him as much as he thought the
lawman had to know, which was simply that he had
been travelling through, had met Evelyn Scott who

needed a rangeboss, and he had decided to take the job.

Marshal Holt was an old hand at his trade. He nodded, accepting all he had been told, then asked another question. 'Where you from, Mister Lane?'

'Montana.'

'Is that a fact? What part?'

'A dinky place called Mandan Prairie.'

The marshal's eyes widened slightly. 'Mandan Prairie? Did you know a cowman up there by the name of Henry Poole, runs cattle over pretty much all that country?'

'He was my father-in-law, Marshal.'

The older man gazed at John Lane for a moment or two in silence before he said, 'That's where I heard the name before. I sort of wondered … you was …'

'I was married to Henry Poole's daughter.'

The marshal barely inclined his head. 'She got taken down a year or so back … what was her name, Mister Lane?'

'Suellen. And she died last summer.'

The law officer looked up at the tall man who was standing nearby. Billy had not returned from out back. 'Jeff, this ain't Barnes. This here is the feller who left the country after Henry Poole's girl died last summer. You remember.'

The tall man did not say whether he remembered or not. He looked solemnly at John Lane then turned on his heel to go out back to see how Billy was.

Marshal Holt shrugged. 'That's his nephew you hit.'

'I was beginnin' to get a little roiled, Marshal.'

'Don't worry. Billy'll get over it. Tell me, Mister Lane, what do you know about the lady who owns this ranch?'

'Not much. Her husband died four years back. A horse fell with him.'

'That's too bad. But it happens.'

'Her rangeboss quit an' when we met on a prairie meadow some time back she offered me the job. I came down here this morning to look the place over. She'd told me she had a smithy, so I shod the horse. That's about all I know, except that she was born about three, four miles from here in a log house.'

The lawman eased back where he was sitting, admired the way the barn was built for a moment, then looked over at John Lane as he said, 'Y'know, if I wanted a place where no one'd find me, this would be it. We had a map – two maps – and we still got lost twice. Not until we rode high up and seen a road, did we find this yard.'

John Lane's hostility had vanished. He rather liked the greying, soft-spoken deputy U.S. Marshal. About the tall man with the dragoon moustache and his nephew he was ambiguous. Neither of them had much of a personality.

When the other two returned to the barn the taller man said, 'Riders, Everett, a hell of a distance off to the northwest. Looks like three.'

The marshal's reply was soft. 'Keep watch. When they're close enough to make out if it's two men an' the lady, let me know.'

After Jeff and Billy went out back again Marshal Holt stood up, worked his legs a little and grimaced. 'You never think it's goin' to happen to you, Mister Lane, but it does. One day you roll out and jump up to pull on your boots, the next morning you roll out, need somethin' to hold to before you can stand up, an' your boots weigh a ton.'

They had established a camaraderie of sorts. The

marshal was an easy man to like. In fact John Lane had met other federal lawmen, badge-heavy individuals which Everett Holt clearly was not. He didn't even sound like someone with authority. He said, 'I was real sorry to hear about Suellen. When she was a little tyke I used to lead her around on my horse.'

John smiled a little and watched the marshal go as far as the rear barn opening. It did not occur to him right then that he could probably get away while their interest was on distant riders. It did occur to him as he sat there, that whoever or whatever Arthur Barnes was, if he knew the federal law was after him, which he probably knew otherwise he wouldn't have been in the mountains and found the Scott ranch where he got hired on with as little chance of being identified and apprehended as any other fugitive, Barnes would be a leery individual. Maybe he would ride right into the yard and be trapped, maybe he might have a hunch, but whatever the fugitive did, he was with the handsome woman. Any attempt at apprehension could, and very likely would, result in a fight. For what Barnes had done he could expect to die in a hell-hole of a prison, or shoot his way clear. Evelyn Scott would be a principal player if he decided to fight clear. Desperate men did desperate things.

John arose, dusted his seat and walked back where the three men were standing motionless and silent. In the distance it was easy to identify one woman rider and two men. John Lane tapped Marshal Holt on the shoulder, jerked his head and waited until the older man had followed then said, 'The woman could get killed.'

Marshal Holt nodded. 'She'll be with 'em for a fact. I'll be here in the barn. Billy an' Jeff'll be across the yard ... Mister Lane, we'll be careful, the rest is up to

Barnes.'

Holt turned to rejoin his companions at the rear barn opening. John strolled without haste, crossed to the smithy, buckled his belt-gun into place and returned.

Out back Jeff said, 'Sure as hell he's one of them, Marshal.'

Holt did not reply. He was leaning in the doorway hidden by shadows. He was unhurried and unhurriedable. He was also unshakably dogged. He had been searching for one of those men out yonder for better than two years. He felt no fear and no elation, just satisfaction that the end of a long trail was close.

FIVE
Waiting

There was something about Marshal Everett Holt the dolorous man called Jeff could have explained to John Lane, except that right at that moment he was too occupied watching approaching riders, and he probably would not have mentioned it anyway.

Everett Holt, an amiable, soft-spoken, pleasant man, possessed two essential elements which make successful lawmen. One, he was like a dog with a bone in its teeth, he absolutely never quit a manhunt until he had been successful. The other attribute was that, as now with the woman riding beside his prey, if the President of the United States had been riding with that fugitive, it would not have made one iota of difference who got hurt as long as Marshal Holt got his man.

When John Lane joined the others at the rear barn opening they did not look around nor notice that he had got his shirt and sidearm from the smithy.

With no advance warning a lobo wolf came out of an arroyo a hundred and fifty feet in front of the approaching trio and ran belly-down in a grey streak for some distant trees. Both riders sprang to the ground, one had a Winchester, the other had only his handgun. They both blazed away which made Evelyn Scott's horse throw a hissy. She rode it out, made it face around where the firing was going on while the uninjured big grey wolf ran for all he was worth.

One of the riders sprang astride. He was the man with the saddlegun. He lit out after the wolf while the woman and remaining rangeman sat and watched.

When the pursuing rider disappeared in the stand of trees where the wolf had sought cover, Marshal Holt said, 'Son of a bitch! That was Barnes.'

Taciturn, dour Jeff nodded his head while Billy neither moved nor agreed. He was intent on watching. John Lane said, 'You can't tell from here, Marshal.'

The older man answered in cold fury. 'When you been on a man's trail as long as I've been on his, Mister Lane, you even know what he eats for breakfast, how he sets a horse, an' what's likely to do. That was Arthur Barnes as sure we're standin' here.'

Billy turned. 'We can run him down.'

The marshal was watching the remaining rider and the woman. They had begun to ride toward the yard again. Wolves were anathema to mountain stockmen. But waiting for the pursuing rider to return wasn't necessary.

'We'll wait for the lady an' the other feller,' the marshal said, peering with narrowed eyes in the direction of the stand of trees where the rider had disappeared. 'Nothin' else we can do. Let 'em ride in, wait until they're on the ground, then Billy, you take their horses. Me'n Jeff will catch them standin' flat-footed.'

John Lane leaned in the rear barn opening. The two oncoming riders were on a slack rein, relaxed and at ease. They conversed a little right up until they came to the yard heading for the tie-rack in front of the barn, and saw an inoffensive, rumpled, harmless-looking older man leaning in the doorway watching them.

Marshal Holt took off his hat to Evelyn Scott as she reined to a halt and swung to the ground. She acknowledged his gallantry by nodding as she held out her reins for the man with her to take – and unsmiling Billy walked out of the barn, took both sets of reins without looking at the woman or her rangeman, led the horses inside as Marshal Holt introduced himself, fumbled until he found the badge and held it for the astonished pair to look at before he pocketed it and spoke in his disarming quiet voice.

He addressed the rider not the woman. 'Mind tellin' me your name, friend?'

The rider answered in a flat tone of voice. 'Bob Lytle.'

Marshal Holt genially smiled. 'Mister Lytle, that feller who went after the wolf – what's his name?'

Evelyn Scott replied in a cold tone of voice. 'His name is Ben Tuttle. What do you want here, Marshal?'

Everett Holt smiled kindly when he replied, 'I want to talk to him.'

'Why, Marshal?'

'You'll be Missus Scott, ma'm?'

'Yes.'

'Well, I just want to talk to that feller is all. In my business we spend a lot of time talkin' to folks who might know something we'd like to know … If you folks'll just step into the barn, we'll just wait for Mister Tuttle.'

The rider, a seamed, weathered older man with a

perpetual squint, looked at his employer and since she had not moved neither did he.

Lanky, sour-looking Jeff stepped into the doorway with both thumbs hooked in his shellbelt and looked gravely at the rider named Bob Lytle.

Evelyn Scott walked into the barn. Lytle followed.

She saw John Lane and gazed steadily at him until Marshal Holt said, 'Him? Mister Lane? He'd just finished shoein' his horse when we come along … I knew his pappy-in-law up in Montana. It's a small world, Miz Scott. Would you care to set on that barrel yonder?'

She regarded Marshal Holt with her pale gaze. 'Would you explain what this is about?' she asked.

Marshal Holt sat on a rail. 'It's about a man named Arthur Barnes, ma'm. He killed a federal messenger some time back an' I've been lookin' for him ever since.'

She did sit, but not on the barrel, on a stool near the harness room. 'You think Arthur Barnes is here on my ranch?'

'I just got to make sure, Miz Scott … about that feller who run after the wolf: How long's he been workin' for you?'

'Five or six years. Why? When was this messenger shot?'

'About that long ago, give or take a year.'

The handsome woman shot John Lane a sulphurous glance then returned her attention to the federal lawman. 'Why here, Mister Holt? What would make you suspect he might be here on my ranch?'

John Lane was interested in this. He leaned on a barn upright waiting while Billy and Jeff finished caring for the horses, and also turned.

Marshal Holt answered in his quiet way, no longer

smiling at the handsome woman. 'Well now, I knew that feller Barnes killed. But that ain't the issue. The issue is a man don't kill a federal messenger, a federal marshal, even a federal teamster, but that the government don't take kindly to such things ... about Barnes, I been lookin' for him off'n on for five years, since he killed that feller. Been to most places he'd been. I talked to a lot of folks who knew him real well. The last place, ma'm, was in a town south of here called Berksville. A storekeeper an' a blacksmith looked at the wanted dodger I been carryin' all them years, and told me they was sure he worked up here on the Scott place; they'd seen him come to town with a wagon a lot of times over the past few years.' Marshal Holt smiled. 'So that's why I'm here. That's why I got to talk to Mister Tuttle. It's the federal law that's involved, ma'm. I'm sure you wouldn't want to do nothin' to make it hard for me, would you?'

Evelyn Scott'd had time to adjust. She ignored John Lane with obvious antagonism. She had her reasons for believing he was part of all this, but right at the moment she looked steadily at the unctuous-acting, soft-spoken federal officer when she replied.

'Ben Tuttle worked for us when my husband was alive. He's never been troublesome, he's a good worker, knows his job and if he's a murderer, Marshal, there has to be more to it than you've said.'

John Lane was watching the rumpled older man, who was regarding the handsome woman. He evidently thought he was up against someone who was hostile because he said, 'Ma'm, I been listenin' for a gun shot. There hasn't been one so I got to figure Mister Tuttle didn't get his wolf. He'll appear out yonder directly now. I'd like your cooperation ... We'll just set in here out of sight, quiet an' all, until he rides into the yard.'

What the handsome woman thought of that was anyone's guess; her expression did not change nor did she speak. She and her rider could have been statues. John Lane admired her toughness. As for the rider, an older man, it was obvious that he respected his boss, female or not.

After some time had passed Jeff came in from out back to tell Marshal Holt there was no sign of Barnes. When Holt said, 'Well, maybe he run that danged wolf a long way,' the sour-faced man shook his head. 'Everett, that wolf's either went to ground or that feller give up on him and had ought to have rode back into sight by now.'

Marshal Holt eyed the other man with squinty little calculating eyes. 'All right. I expect if you'n Billy went out there … He's goin' to see you sure as the devil. You got to make it believable that you're just a grub-liner or a feller who got lost up in here. You got to get real close, Jeff. Barnes is a bad man with weapons.'

After the dour man had gone out back to gather Billy for the manhunt Marshal Holt got more comfortable. With time to kill and, as yet, no real reason to worry, he became jolly again. He asked Bob Lytle how long he'd been riding for the Holt outfit. When Lytle told him the marshal's smile turned ingratiating. 'When I've rode with a man as long as you've rode with Mister Tuttle, it just come naturally the fellers talked. About growin' up back in Missouri or somewhere. What they done in the lives …'

Evidently Bob Lytle was no novice. He looked steadily at the lawman when he said, 'I never asked questions and he never volunteered anything except that he'd been a rider in Wyoming. Never mentioned where he come from. Never talked about personal things.'

Marshal Holt put his head slightly to one side as he regarded the rangeman. 'Not once in five years, friend?'

'Not that I can recall, Marshal. We got to be pretty good friends. I can't recall him ever ....'

'Miz Scott? Mister Tuttle ever take his hair down a little around you?'

Evelyn Scott gently wagged her head. 'No. Never.' She had already done what John Lane had only just begun to understand. The rumpled, genial, greying man with the badge in his pocket was not what he seemed to be.

But Everett Holt was an accomplished actor. John Lane had never seen a lawman like Holt before. He was fascinated but the handsome woman clearly was not.

She said, 'Marshal, you can't expect a person to enjoy being a captive in their own yard.'

Marshal Holt spread his hands, smiled his most disarming smile. 'You ain't a prisoner, ma'm,' he said. 'You're a decent law-abidin' lady helpin' the law.'

'In that case, if you'll excuse me ...' She stood up.

Holt's smile remained but it was no longer disarming. 'Set back down, ma'm.' That was all he said but to John Lane the older man's softly spoken words had a ring of steel to them.

The handsome woman did not sit down, for a long moment, then she did. Now her gaze, her entire expression was hostile, which Marshal Holt had no doubt expected because when he spoke again, the voice remained almost a drawl, it was as quiet as always, but what he said was very much to the point.

'Lady, I put too much time into findin' Barnes to let anyone – not even a real nice-lookin' woman like you

– keep me from tying him belly-down for the ride back, if that's the way he wants it. We'll just set. It shouldn't be much longer.'

John Lane stepped to the back barn opening to scan the countryside. There was no sign of Billy and his uncle. Lane leaned back there, rolled and lighted a smoke and had little difficulty imagining why the handsome woman's attitude had changed so abruptly toward him.

Marshal Holt's call scattered John Lane's thoughts. 'Mister Lane, I'd take it kindly if you'd come back where we are.' There was no threat in the voice, no command, but John Lane knew better than to disobey. He killed the smoke and returned to the pleasant, fragrant interior of the old barn. For the first time since Evelyn Scott had met the lawman, she put a deliberate, slightly puzzled gaze on John Lane. He shrugged very slightly and sat on the opposite side of the barn runway a yard or so from Marshal Holt.

The marshal produced a massive gold watch, opened the face, regarded the spidery black hands a moment, snapped the case closed and re-pocketed the watch. He puckered his brow slightly. 'Them boys been gone quite a spell,' he said more to himself than to the others. Bob Lytle made a comment about that. 'From where we jumped that wolf, mister, it's a fair distance to the bottom of that Castle Rock. Farther than a man'd think.'

Marshal Holt nodded about that. 'You're likely right, Mister Lytle. What I was thinkin' there's been no gun shot.' All three people with the lawman looked long and thoughtfully at him. He had expected shooting? In that case what he'd said about wanting to talk to the fugitive was a lie. He wanted the fugitive dead *or* alive. Probably mostly dead.

Evelyn Scott asked a question. 'Suppose you're wrong, Marshal?' She was poised to say more but his smile appeared before she had the opportunity.

'Ma'm, not this time. Not with Arthur Barnes.'

'Then when you sent those two men to find him ...?'

'Lady, I *know* all I got to know about Barnes. I'll take him face down or sittin' up, I'm not making no mistake. Not with this one. There's nothin' he can tell me I don't already know. He'd just lie a blue streak anyway.'

Bob Lytle put a quizzical look upon John Lane, who understood the look but did not respond to it. He was wondering about something else. Several hours had passed. At least one hour had passed since the handsome woman and her rider had ridden into the yard. Any time he'd chased wolves he had either shot them or they had escaped in something like fifteen, maybe twenty minutes. Could the man Marshal Holt had so relentlessly tracked down got the wind about danger in the yard?

Evidently Everett Holt was beginning to wonder the same thing, because he stood up, smoothed his rumpled coat, raised both arms to re-set his hat – and John Lane saw something that held his attention. Marshal Holt did not wear the customary shellbelt and holstered Colt. He had one of those new-fangled double action Colts with the kind of handles some folks called a 'parrot beak'. The handles had ivory grips. It was in a holster attached to the lawman's britches belt, covered by the marshal's baggy old coat.

John Lane thought the lawman would not be able to get at his weapon with any kind of speed. On the other hand, Everett Holt looked to be well along, and he had said or implied he had been a federal officer for many years; anyone following his kind of work and was as old as Marshal Holt looked to be, had certainly run against gunmen, at the very least very desperate fugitives.

John arose to walk to the front barn opening. He leaned there looking across the serene yard. The big old dog was stretched out like a rug on the verandah of the main-house.

This was the damnedest affair he'd ever been involved in being played out in the most peaceful setting he had ever seen.

He turned. The handsome woman was looking in his direction. She was, as usual, expressionless otherwise he might have offered an encouraging smile.

He returned to his seat near the marshal as Bob Lytle evidently could not resist. He said, 'Mister Holt, them friends of yours been gone long enough to be half way up the trail to Castle Rock.'

Holt sighed, consulted his watch again, leaned as far as he had to in order to look at the sky, leaned back and regarded the cowboy without smiling. 'You'n Mister Barnes see us here, did you, Mister Lytle?'

'When we was out yonder all we saw was the wolf. I didn't see anyone in the yard until we rode into it.'

'Well then, tell me, Mister Lytle, where do you think Mister Tuttle went? Hell man, he's been gone over two hours. If he'd figured to kill the wolf or lost it, he sure as hell would have come into sight by now.'

Lytle made a small, humourless grin. 'Seems like he would, don't it? But your friends'll find him. He sure don't expect no lawman to be up in here.'

'You're sure of that, are you?'

Evelyn Scott broke into this discussion. 'Are you

implying that we somehow knew you were here, and told Ben to run for it?'

Instead of replying, Marshal Holt arose and went to the rear barn opening. He stood back there for a long time, half sideways so he could at the same time keep an eye on the people he'd left.

John Lane and the handsome woman gazed at each other. She remained expressionless. He had no idea what she was thinking, but when he looked away, over where Bob Lytle was leaning, the rangeman slowly dropped one eyelid and raised it.

SIX
A Night To Remember

John Lane had to wonder what the rangeman's sly wink meant. If his first notion was correct, then somehow or other either the handsome woman or Bob Lytle knew something about Tuttle's disappearance.

How they could possibly know a federal lawman was waiting for Barnes-Tuttle, or whatever his name was, in the yard on this particular day, so many years after a crime had been committed, completely escaped him.

He was hungry. Slackening thirst was no problem although someone watched everything he did. He had already resolved some of the hunger with smokes, but they were neither as satisfactory for his purpose as just plain drinking water had been.

When an increasingly anxious federal marshal returned to stand sideways looking across the empty land where shadows were assuming more depth and colour, John Lane looked at Evelyn Scott and shook his head.

She turned away.

Bob Lytle looked mildly amused, but none of them could speak their minds with Marshal Holt within earshot.

The huge old dog came ambling down to join the people in the barn. Marshal Holt turned, watched for a moment before asking the handsome woman if it was feeding time. She was scratching the dog when she replied. 'Yes. Past his feeding time.'

Holt returned his gaze to the empty land which was steadily working its way toward dusk. He did something John Lane had not seen him do before, he fished in one of his baggy coat pockets, brought forth a cut plug and gnawed off a corner. He then expectorated once and did not do it again for as long as cud was in his cheek.

John Lane ambled back to join the vigil. Marshal Holt spoke in an almost comradely fashion. 'They got to be comin' back. They been gone long enough for Barnes to have got clear, or for them to have caught the bastard.'

John Lane could not dispute that. He rolled and lighted a quirley before saying, 'How long can you go without feeding?'

Holt did not look away from his distant scanning as he replied. 'As long as I got to.'

'Suppose they got lost, Marshal.'

This time the lawman put a slow, annoyed look on his companion at the rear barn opening. 'They won't get lost. Hell man, Jeff was a tracker for the army. You couldn't lose him.'

John Lane came right back. 'In that case, they've either found whatever-his-name-is, or he's caught them.'

Evidently the older man had considered these possibilities. 'Mister Lane, I don't figure there's a man in the territory who could out-figure Jeff on a manhunt. I've known him a lot of years.'

'Is he also a federal officer?'

Holt was back to watching, only now his eyes were squinted as though in some way that aided dusk-vision. 'Naw, Jeff's just an old friend. When I can I give 'em a little work. Him an' Billy, his nephew ... By the way, Mister Lane, Billy's not the kind to forget gettin' hit.'

Lane leaned to also look northwesterly. He said, 'He'd be wise if he did, Marshal. Lots of things in this life a man'd be wise just to forget ... It wasn't my idea him gettin' his hackles up.'

'... Mister Lane, look sharp almost due north – is that somethin' movin' out there?'

John stepped clear of the barn facing northward. He nodded slowly. 'It sure is, Mister Holt ... It's driftin' cattle.'

The lawman leaned on the side of the opening, finally now he was worried. There were no more excuses that would explain his missing companions – and the outlaw.

He mused aloud. 'If it was daylight I could ride out there.'

John Lane said nothing about that, but he did mention his hunger, which Marshal Holt appeared not to have heard.

Holt returned to the darkening interior of the barn and stood before Evelyn Scott. 'How did you do it? We'll get him. If we got to track him to hell an' for two days over the coals, we'll get him. Tell me straight out, lady, how did you warn him off? Now, don't tell you or this feller who rides for you, didn't, because that's the only way Barnes could have run off. If, some way, he was warned ... My professional interest is aroused, ma'm. How did you do it?'

He might as well have addressed a stone. John Lane saw the handsome woman's eyes raise slowly to meet the gaze of the marshal. She did not make any attempt to speak, in fact she scornfully turned away.

John Lane wondered if she hadn't made a mistake. Marshal Holt hadn't smiled nor used his usual ingratiating tone in more than an hour.

The lawman stood a moment looking at the woman, then turned toward her rider, who had also been listening and watching. Before the lawman spoke Bob Lytle held up a hand. 'He wasn't warned, Marshal. How could we have warned him about you when we didn't know you was in the country?'

Holt pulled his coat back to plunge both hands into the pockets of his trousers. He looked steadily at the rangeman. They were very likely about the same age.

Lytle was a needler. He had needled the lawman before. Now he did it again. 'You don't expect them friends of yours rode down Ben's rifle barrel do you? That'd account for them not comin' back, an' it'd also account for no gunfire, wouldn't it?'

Marshal Holt did not look like he even knew how to smile, but his voice was still soft. 'Jeff an' his nephew, especially Jeff, is good sign readers, Mister Lytle. They know who they're after. Barnes ain't goin' to catch them out. Not by a damned sight.'

Lytle still faintly smiled as he did it again. 'Marshal, Ben Tuttle knows every nook an' cranny of the Scott range. If somethin' spooked him, I don't care how *coyote* your friends are, if Ben don't want to be caught, he ain't going to be caught.'

That remark brought the discussion back where it had started. Marshal Holt still faced the rangeman. John Lane again expected the explosion. Maybe the older man wouldn't be violent toward a woman, but Bob Lytle didn't fit that category, and for a fact he had stung the federal officer several times.

Marshal Holt extended his left hand. His right hand was still in the pocket under his coat. 'Give me your gun,' he said to the rangeman. Bob Lytle crossed both arms across his chest. 'Take it,' he said. John Lane thought the fight was now imminent, but again he was wrong. Out of nowhere and with so little motion the coat seemed hardly to have moved, the double-action Colt revolver was out and aimed. Marshal Holt drew back the hammer. 'Give me the gun, Mister Lytle.'

Evelyn Scott broke in. 'Give him the gun, Bob. It's not worth getting shot about.'

Lytle handed over the weapon, Holt stepped back before holstering his own weapon. He looked sideways at John Lane, then at the seated woman before speaking.

'I'm goin' to find out how it was done if I got to do some overhauling.'

Lytle's gun in the lawman's fist swivelled without haste until the snout was aimed squarely at John Lane's soft parts. 'Empty the holster, Mister Lane … Don't make me do somethin' I'll regret, because someday I'll see your pappy-in-law an' I don't want to tell him I shot you. *Drop it!*'

Lane let the gun fall. Holt motioned for him to kick it over, which Lane did, but the lawman made no attempt to pick it up, he waggled the gun in his fist toward the area where Evelyn Scott was sitting. They obediently went over there, then Bob Lytle had to needle the older man again.

He said, 'Mister Holt, you're ridin' a lame horse. Any way you look at it – them friends of yours ain't comin' back, you made me'n Mister Barnes annoyed at you – an' with night comin' that feller you're lookin' for is likely as not to come slippin' back in the dark for his gatherings. Nights get awful cold in this country, Marshal. Specially in big old draughty barns.'

Holt growled for the first time since he and John Lane had met. 'Set down an' shut up,' he told Bob Lytle, who obliged with a faintly taunting smile.

The big dog growled. They looked at him. He was facing the front of the barn, the big tree-shadowed yard, his back straight, his ears forward when he growled deep in his throat.

Marshal Holt let the barrel of the gun droop as he asked Evelyn Scott what the dog could be upset about. She shrugged. 'Bear scent, wolf scent, cougar scent – maybe your friends coming back,'

'Or Barnes,' the lawman exclaimed.

She shook her head. 'He knows Ben Tuttle too well. He's very fond of Ben.'

John Lane was sitting relaxed. As long as the federal officer was easy and amiable, it had not seemed that their situation was too bad, but since being needled by Bob Lytle, the marshal's calm, sly amiability had seemed to evaporate.

As far as John Lane was concerned, there was only one of two ways this affair could end, and it seemed to him neither of those ways posed a real peril to the people in the barn with Marshal Holt, so he leaned back against wood and quietly said, 'Roast turkey, stuffed mallard, a medium steak big as a hat ...'

Marshal Holt ignored Lane.

Bob Lytle took it up. 'Me, I'm partial to fat pork with pepper gravy over a dozen biscuits, an' coffee hot enough to scald a cat.'

Holt looked steadily at them, judging from his expression his thoughts were not friendly. Twice he arose, went out back standing sideways so he could simultaneously look back inside the barn and out across the land. Visibility was getting increasingly bad, inside the barn and outside it. The last time Holt made that trip and returned to his seat on the rail, he said, 'I'm not goin' back without him.' He left it up to the others to guess who he meant. They had no difficulty. The dog growled deep in its throat, not a very friendly sound. John Lane watched the animal. Since his arrival in the yard he and the dog had gotten along very well. It would have been hard for John to imagine the big friendly dog seriously growling, but that is exactly what he was doing.

As time passed and darkness came closer none of the people in the barn had much doubt that Jeff and Billy had found their man – or he had found them.

Evelyn Scott stood up resolutely. 'I'm going to the house,' she told the marshal. 'You can shoot me in the back if you wish, but I've had enough of sitting in here.'

The lawman had moments to make his decision. It was not to shoot the woman in the back. He stood up, growled Lane and Lytle to their feet, and herded them ahead of him in the direction of the main-house with the handsome woman about twenty feet ahead.

The dog brought up the rear, occasionally raising its massive head to sniff the descending night, but it did not growl.

Inside, the handsome woman lighted lamps. Her hired rider went to kneel at the fireplace and painstakingly select only fat wood to start the fire. It was chilly in the house, and draughty. Marshal Holt told Evelyn to stay in the parlour with the others. She seemed to John Lane about to refuse when the dog began growling again outside on the porch. This time his owner put her head slightly to one side, listened briefly and made a statement. 'It is definitely not Ben.'

She went to the edge of a window so that she would

not be backgrounded, and looked out. The three men watched. Marshal Holt also got into shadows. He had the sixgun aimed squarely at the door.

The handsome woman faced him. 'It has two legs, whoever it is. Shep has a different growl for people than he has for animals.'

'How close are your neighbours?' the lawman asked.

'About six miles closer to town. But it's not them, they always holler to let us know they're coming.'

Marshal Holt switched his appropriated sixgun from one hand to the other. Sweaty palms were a nuisance.

John Lane watched the federal officer, who hadn't smiled nor spoken since entering the house.

John Lane thought that the federal officer's nerves were crawling, and in a way he did not blame Holt, they were only the good Lord knew how far from help.

The dog's noise subsided only to be resumed after a long interval. Marshal Holt made an unkind remark. 'If that dog belonged to me I'd shoot him.'

The handsome woman turned on him, surprising John Lane with her temper. 'A watch dog watches,' she told the marshal. 'Shep is one of the best watch dogs we've ever had. If you shoot my dog, Marshal, I'll bury you at the base of the cliff.'

She had spoken as though she meant every word, which John Lane was certain she did. How she could accomplish the threat he had no idea, but he nodded admiringly at her when the scolding ended because Marshal Holt became his practiced easy-going grandfather type again.

'Just a manner of speakin', ma'm. I've never shot a dog in my life.'

Shep was growling again but making no move like other dogs would have done. He remained on the porch.

Evelyn went to her kitchen and fired up the cook stove. She too was hungry. Marshal Holt put up the gun, sauntered to the kitchen doorway and smilingly watched the handsome woman work. He said. 'I expect you're a good cook, ma'm.'

She ignored him as she got busy making a meal, right up until he said, 'Your husband was a lucky man, havin' a purty wife, a good cook an' all.'

The cowboy and John Lane were listening in the parlour, the cowboy gave John Lane an ironic look, lowered his voice to say, 'He's wastin' his time. That there is a one-man woman an' she buried him some time back.'

Evelyn Scott turned from the cupboard where she was getting dishes, gazed coldly at the federal marshal and said, 'My husband was a good man, Mister Holt. He never hunted people down nor sat in judgment on them. He was kindly and. ... I'm wasting my breath.' She went back to removing dishes from the cupboard, her back as straight as a ramrod.

The marshal leaned, watched for a while, then spoke again, his voice soft. 'Lady, I never hunted a man down unless he had it comin'. I never used my gun unless the other feller deserved it.'

From the parlour the rangeman did it again. He said, 'Shootin' folks because they deserved it ain't exactly what the law says justifies killin', does it?'

John Lane tensed as the older man slowly turned, put his steady gaze on Bob Lytle, waited a moment then said, 'Mister Lytle, you're beginnin' to upset me.'

John Lane hoped very hard the rangeman would let it lie, but that wasn't Lytle's nature. 'Well now,

Mister Holt, that wasn't my intention ... I was just wonderin' how many folks you shot because you figured they deserved it.'

John Lane felt like hitting the cowboy. Marshal Holt continued to gaze at Lytle. After another pause he spoke again. 'No more'n I had to, Mister Lytle. I been at this business about as long as you are old. Maybe not quite that long, but it's a line of work where a man's got to defend himself now'n then.'

The handsome woman stopped this by asking the marshal how he liked his meat cooked. Holt faced her with his unctuous smile, 'Rare, ma'm, if it ain't too much trouble.'

She stepped past Holt and glared at her rider, turned back to the stove and resumed making their meal.

There was no more conversation for a long time, until the dog on the porch began growling again deep in his throat, and continued to do it. John Lane stepped over beside a window, but it was as dark as the inside of a boot. He returned to a chair as Marshal Holt said, 'Jeff an' Billy, more'n likely. He'd growl at them I expect.'

Evelyn called them to the kitchen table. John Lane swept past the lawman and sat down. He and the handsome woman exchanged a look. Lane said, 'I haven't eaten since Molly an' I had breakfast.'

Marshal Holt was sitting at the table when he asked who Molly was. Lane told him. The marshal stared at the younger man. 'A tame bear? A cub, Mister Lane?'

Evelyn cut in. 'No, she is old now. She weighs about four hundred pounds. I had her for a playmate when I was growing up.'

Marshal Holt speared a steak, watched the drippings before putting it on his plate. It was rare.

As he reached for the salt he said, 'Ma'm, a bear ain't nothin' to get friendly with. You can't ever tell what they're goin' to do.'

Evelyn did not respond. She sat, waited until the platter came her way then helped herself to a well-done piece of meat. Bob Lytle was another rare-meat man. John Lane wasn't particular. He'd been hungry so long he'd have eaten the rear end out of a bob cat if someone would hold its head.

The dog growled menacingly again, a deeper, more serious sound. Whatever was out in the night he did not like even a little.

Marshal Holt listened, went back to eating as he said, 'If it's Jeff an' Billy most likely what's takin' them so long is tyin' the prisoner an' carin' for the horses.'

John Lane looked at the lawman. Holt was attacking his food, evidently he hadn't eaten in a while too.

Bob Lytle made what seemed a harmless remark. 'If it was your friends, Marshal, they'd have enough sense to holler out, wouldn't they? Let you know they're back?'

Marshal Holt slowly put down his eating utensils, leaned back and was about to speak when the handsome woman spoke first. 'Bob, stop that!'

Lytle ducked his head and concentrated on his meal. The only sound was the growling big dog. When John Lane had taken the edge off his appetite he abruptly arose and passed through the parlour to open the door and look out. Marshal Holt spoke quietly from the kitchen. 'Don't go no farther, Mister Lane.'

The light was poor inside but much poorer outside. Without any warning a gun flashed in the area of the barn. John Lane felt as though the breath had been knocked out of him, he held fast to the door as he was punched backwards, was still clinging to the door as he sank to his knees, then lost his grip on the door and fell forward.

The three people at the kitchen table sprang up simultaneously. Evelyn Scott and her rider crossed the parlour, pulled Lane inside and closed the door.

Marshal Holt stood in the kitchen doorway. When they rolled John Lane onto his back the lawman came closer, sucked his teeth a moment and said, 'I expect that'll be Mister Barnes out there.' He squinted at the leaking blood and added a little more. 'Dang poor light to shoot by ... I'd guess Mister Barnes thought Mister Lane was me. We're about the same height an' heft. Now then, if Mister Barnes is loose, why then I'd figure Jeff an' Billy is also out there; can't track him in the dark but they'll have heard that gunshot.'

The handsome woman put one of her sulphurous looks at the marshal as she said, 'Bob, take his feet, I'll take his shoulders.' As Marshal Holt would have helped she swore at him. 'Get the hell away! You've caused enough grief for one day. Go back and finish your supper.'

SEVEN
The Stalker

They carried Lane to a rear bedroom with a musty smell as though it hadn't been used lately. They placed him on the bed as Evelyn Scott told her rider to fetch a lamp. When she and the federal marshal were alone she unbuckled Lane's shellbelt with its empty holster, removed it and straightened up peering at her fingers, they were sticky wet but without light she could only guess the cause.

When Lytle returned with two lamps and put them nearby the handsome woman bent for a closer look. Night-shooting was never predictable, nor very accurate. The bullet had hit the buckle of John Lane's shellbelt, had shattered it but had flattened against the trouser belt behind the first buckle.

She peeled away the torn shirt, soggy with blood, leaned down again to assess the injury and slowly plucked the trouser belt away, examined it and held it for her rider to see.

The slug had shattered. Most of the lead was welded to the second buckle but shards of lead had torn the skin. She said, 'Mister Holt, there's some sulphur powder mixed with alum behind you on the dresser in a blue bottle – if you please.'

While she was caring for the unconscious man's wound Everett Holt said, 'I never heard of a man gettin' a little hit like that an' losin' consciousness.'

The handsome woman raised her eyes. Whether she was going to speak or not the sound of a running horse distracted her. It also distracted Marshal Holt, who swore with feeling. 'The son of a bitch is gettin' away!'

Evelyn Scott said, 'Go after him.'

Holt seemed to teeter between courses of action, before he said, 'No, we'll get him. We come pretty close before. We'll run the bastard down. I'm used to this sort of thing.'

The handsome woman and her rider ignored the lawman. She told Lytle what to do and he did it without speaking. Bandaging the injury after it had been cleansed required strength. They had to lift John Lane to get the bandaging under and around him. Marshal Holt watched, said nothing, and eventually sought relief from frustration by tucking a cud into his cheek.

Lytle spoke as he and his employer were bending over the man on the bed. 'Marshal, I got a question you can maybe he'p me with. If that wasn't Ben out there, an' I doubt that it was, then why did someone try to shoot you, thinkin' Mister Lane was you?'

Holt scowled. 'What kind of tomfoolishness is that? It was Barnes, believe me it was. He come back for his gatherings an' …'

Lytle did it again, but this driving a wedge instead of simply taunting the lawman. 'Naw; like I said, I rode with Ben Tuttle some years. If he knew you was here, even if he caught your friends an' left 'em out yonder somewhere, he wouldn't come back just for a razor an' a bedroll if he knew his life was in the balance. Ben's no fool, Mister Holt.'

Evelyn Scott said, 'Bob, leave it be. Fetch the brandy

from the kitchen.' After Lytle departed the handsome woman straightened up looking stonily at Marshal Holt.

'Why would Ben Tuttle waste time trying to shoot you? Like Bob said, he is no fool. If he came back to the yard for his gatherings or maybe a fresh horse, his idea would be to leave the country the fastest way he could, which would mean in darkness without making any more noise than he had to.'

'Lady,' responded the lawman. 'You heard that runnin' horse. He *is* gettin' away.'

Lytle returned with the bottle. Evelyn said no more, she and her rider raised John Lane, got him to swallow three times then eased him back down. As she handed the bottle to her rider she again addressed the lawman. 'I know him, Marshal. So does Bob. Ben Tuttle wouldn't have risked getting shot or caught by trying to kill you. He'd run for it, put as much territory between the two of you as he could.'

Marshal Holt leaned on the wall. Only one thing they had said fit what he knew about his prey. The man they knew as Ben Tuttle was motivated to flee as far and as fast as he could. That would for a fact be his primary concern. In fact it would be the primary concern of any outlaw.

Something else occurred to the federal lawman. If that had been Barnes trying to kill him, where in hell were Jeff and Billy? If they had been close enough to have heard that gunshot, by now they should be banging on the door, or racing in pursuit of the bushwhacker.

John Lane's slow recovery, attributable to brandy, caught and held the attention of the handsome woman and her rider, but the attention of the troubled lawman whose reflections had been becoming increasingly gloomy as time passed and neither of his companions had returned, ignored Lane.

He watched the woman and her companion hoist Lane to get another couple of swallows of brandy down him. As they eased him down again, his eyes were watering. Brandy was an excellent way to clear tear ducts.

Bob Lytle eyed the anxious older man. 'You could go out there,' he said. 'If the feller who thought he'd shot you is gone, an' maybe your friends come back ...'

Evelyn Scott faced her rider. Lytle became busy wrapping what was left of the bandaging cloth; he did not meet her cold stare.

The man on the bed spoke. 'Where was I hit?'

Evelyn explained, held up the buckle with the flattened lead on it. John Lane looked at the ruined buckle. 'No wonder I got a stomach ache,' he told them, and felt gingerly where the bandage was. He turned his head, met the gaze of Marshal Holt, looked away and sighed, something which brought instantaneous pain.

Outside, the big dog barked and kept it up. Previously, although the dog had worried the people in the house, this time his barking, which was loud, deep and fierce-sounding, caused all three of them to straighten up listening. Bob Lytle seemed about to say something when he saw the handsome woman regarding him. He sheepishly smiled.

A rock hit the front of the house. They listened to it rattle on the porch. Dogs could not throw rocks. Marshal Holt pulled the appropriated sixgun from his waistband but otherwise remained where he was. After the silence had run on again he spoke to the woman. 'Barnes run off, did he?'

She ignored the sarcasm in the remark, gathered up what they had used on the wounded man and would have left the room but the marshal told her to stay where she was.

She sat on a little chair looking stonily at Everett Holt. Bob Lytle leaned on the wall scowling. For the first time he was having trouble believing that was his riding partner out there.

John Lane broke the stillness. 'Who is out there?'

When neither of the men replied the handsome woman did. 'I don't know, but it's not Ben Tuttle.'

The marshal spoke waspishly. 'Stop callin' him that. His name's Arthur Barnes.'

Her reply was dead calm. 'I doubt it, Mister Holt. If he came back for a fresh horse … You heard that running horse.'

The dog had stopped barking, the house creaked and groaned as the temperature dropped, the light in the bedroom shone steadily, except for one lengthy moment when the flame fluttered.

They all saw that. At least one of them, the woman who had lived for years in the house, stiffened where she sat. Over the years whenever anyone had opened or closed a window or a door, the lamps flickered. She looked at her rider. He looked back from an expressionless face.

The lawman shifted hands with the heavy revolver, slid the sweaty palm down the side of his trousers. In the lamplight he looked different, flame from the lamps made shadow beneath his eyes and etched every line deeper. He looked evil.

John Lane raised up, flinched and propped his head on one hand. Evelyn Scott told him to lie back down, the bleeding would start. He regarded her steadily before speaking.

'I got the feeling in the barn you thought I was part of this.'

She said nothing but he had her attention.

'You told me to come down here when I said my horse needed shoeing, so I came.'

She nodded a little. 'Yes, and when you came to the yard from the south, and those other three came from the north and east, it closed off the yard so that Ben Tuttle couldn't have got away, didn't it?'

John Lane's eyes widened. 'If I was one of them, why would the marshal take my gun an' make me a prisoner like he did you an' your rider?' John Lane jerked his head in the lawman's direction. 'Ask him if he ever saw me before today.'

She moved her gaze to the lawman. He was standing with his head slightly cocked, listening. She did not address him, she returned her gaze to John Lane, and shrugged, which was not good enough, John Lane was indignant. 'Lady, think back, if I'd been one of them would they have treated me like they did? I was in the barn when they came up on my blind side. I watched for the three of you to ride to the yard out back. It wasn't until your rider chased that wolf into the timber that the marshal began acting different. Up to then I guess he figured I was harmless ... Marshal ...?'

Holt held up a hand and wagged his head at them. He was listening more intently now. They watched and also listened. The trouble was that the old house creaked, making it impossible to determine whether someone was inside stalking them, or it was their imaginations.

Marshal Holt swapped hands with the sixgun again. He now had no interest in the others. He tiptoed to the door and stood just inside along the wall as though he expected someone to appear, which did not happen.

Bob Lytle was watching the lawman with coldly amused eyes, but he kept silent. John Lane's middle bothered enough to make him lie down again, but he did not take his eyes off the doorway.

The dog was no longer barking so the silence was complete until another rock struck the front of the house with considerable force. Whoever had hurled it this time was much closer to the house.

Marshal Holt loosened a little. Whoever was doing that had to still be outside. Bob Lytle did it again when he said, 'One outside, one inside. The one outside is to keep us guessin' while his friend works his way inside.'

Evelyn Scott glared, but Lytle was watching the door and missed her expression of disapproval. John Lane asked the federal officer if that could be Jeff or Billy. Holt snorted without bothering to reply. John Lane said, 'Well, it's somebody, ain't it?'

'Barnes,' hissed the marshal.

No one commented.

To John Lane it seemed obvious that whoever had thrown those rocks had done so because they wanted Marshal Holt to know they were out there. He could imagine no other reason for someone to do something like that. The man Evelyn Scott called Tuttle and the lawman said was named Barnes?

If it was, then he had somehow taken care of Holt's companions and had come back for the marshal, which might be the case, depending on how badly the fugitive hated his pursuer. But neither the woman or her rider believed it would be the fugitive, and that left the field of speculation wide open.

Holt abruptly said, 'He's taken care of your dog, lady.'

Evelyn said nothing.

Moments later the dog barked, but only briefly, then growled a few times and finally also stopped that. Bob Lytle said, 'He's made up with Shep, which ain't hard to do.'

John Lane spoke. 'Where is he?'

'Inside or awful close,' the rider stated, seeming to relish the idea. 'Shep was lyin' on the porch.'

Holt made an exclamatory swear word then said, 'Why don't he just yell out? I'll give him a break.'

Again silence settled as three people gazed at the older man over along the front wall near the door.

Marshal Holt suddenly yelled. 'I'm in here, the back bedroom, an' I'm waitin', you son of a bitch.'

There was no reply, only creaking wood making small sounds throughout the house.

Holt turned slitted eyes toward the bed. 'Get out of there,' he snarled at John Lane. 'Get out of there an' walk down the hall toward the parlour. If he figured you was me the first time, he might step out where I can see him the second time.'

Evelyn Scott sprang to her feet, glaring. 'He can't leave that bed,' she exclaimed. 'He couldn't walk the length of that hall without help … If you're not a coward, Mister Holt, go down the hall yourself.'

Marshal Holt turned on her. 'I never been afraid in my life,' he exclaimed, and Bob Lytle, over against the far wall rolled his eyes skyward and gently shook his head.

This time the reaction was positive and swift. Marshal Holt raised and cocked the sixgun aiming directly at the rangeman.

Evelyn stepped between them looking steadily at Marshal Holt. She did not say a word. Their eyes duelled for a moment, until another rock struck the house and distracted them.

Holt cocked his head to listen again. Bob Lytle would have made another sarcastic remark but both the woman and John Lane were glaring at him.

Holt said, 'If he expects me to open that door like Mister Lane done, he'll have a long wait.' Holt slowly looked around at the others. 'If he thinks he shot me in the doorway, why is he keepin' this up?'

No one replied.

The marshal sagged against the wall. He was not a young man and hadn't been one in quite a while, but right now he looked even older. John Lane regarded the older man pensively. When they had first met and for several hours afterward, Everett Holt had seemed kindly, then unctuous and ingratiating, then unsettled and worried until right now he looked and acted like a different human being altogether.

Someone or some thing scraped along the rear of the house, the people inside held their breath. The scraping seemed to John Lane to be made by someone dragging a stick along the wall out back. He looked at Bob Lytle then at the handsome woman, they were too intent to notice until the scraping sound ended then Lytle made one of his dry comments. 'Well, he ain't inside.'

John Lane added one word. 'Yet.'

Marshal Holt sank down on a chair, this was clearly something he'd never encountered before – someone making no secret of his presence in the night: someone who was deliberately demoralising the people inside. The lawman made a frustrated remark that no one heeded. He said, 'That damned dog. Why ain't he growling?'

Evelyn Scott answered matter-of-factly. 'Once you've met him, maybe scratched him, he accepts you.

He's always been that way.'

John Lane agreed with that in silence. He looked at Evelyn and asked if she had a gun in the house. Marshal Holt came to life about that. 'Ma'm, you stay right where you are.'

Bob Lytle felt his empty holster. 'Marshal, maybe he ain't after you. Maybe he's a renegade after somethin' else, like maybe money.'

Everett Holt pushed tiredly up to his feet. To John Lane he seemed to be susceptible to what was happening, perhaps more so than he would have been in broad daylight with a target.

One thing John Lane – they all knew now – the rumpled, soft-speaking older man might look like someone's old harmless grandfather, but he was deadly fast with that double-action Colt.

Lane looked steadily at the lawman, this had nothing to do with Barnes. Someone was after the marshal, someone who had, or at least thought he had, a very good reason for stalking him.

To test this idea John Lane asked the marshal a question. 'You been at this manhunting business a long time, Marshal?'

'Long enough, Mister Lane.'

'In your line of work a man'd would make enemies. Whoever is out there, Mister Holt, has maybe been on your trail as long as you've been on Barnes's trail. Do you think that might be it?'

Marshal Holt's brows dropped, his eyes narrowed on John Lane. 'How would he know I was here?'

'Same way you knew Barnes was here – following, asking questions, not giving up. Mister Holt, can you think of someone who'd want a piece of your hide that bad?'

Marshal Holt shoved the sixgun into the waistband

of his britches, ignored the man in the bed to cross silently to the wall beside the doorway and lean there listening.

The silence was ongoing. Whoever was out there seemed to be in no hurry. He obviously wanted the people inside to sweat, which they were doing.

Holt yelled again, 'If you got the guts come in here where I can see you.'

This time there was a very human response. Someone laughed without a shred of humour. It was a chilling, deadly sound. It lingered as a silent echo in the heads of those who had heard it.

Evelyn spoke. 'How does he know he didn't shoot you, Marshal?'

Bob Lytle answered drily. 'A shot-man don't call out real loud, ma'm, an' if it's like Mister Lane figures, it's someone huntin' the marshal down, chances are he knows his voice when he hears it.'

EIGHT
Death

John Lane's stomach was bothering him. It was less an actual pain than it was a sensation of injured muscles. His face was flushed, his eyes were bright. Brandy burned like fire going down but there was no way to denigrate its immediate uplifting sensation.

As long as the effect of the brandy lasted he would be less aware of his sore middle than he would be after the effect wore off.

This other thing transcended his sense of physical discomfort, and the brandy may have helped here too because he said something the others had more reason to believe the rangerider would say.

'No one lives forever, Marshal. The few lawmen I've known didn't last nearly as long as you have.'

Evelyn looked at Lane in mild surprise but her hired rider smiled.

Marshal Holt cast a withering glance in John Lane's direction. 'I was goin' strong when you was born, Mister Lane, an' I'll be goin' strong after you're gone.'

Their tormentor had been quiet so long Marshal Holt began to feel hopeful. It was dark out there and it was cold.

Evidently he hadn't departed; someone gave a

81

startled outcry which seemed to come from down near the barn. The big dog, probably roused from slumber, made a few half-hearted growls then went silent.

Holt told the others that howl hadn't been made by the man who had laughed. If the others were sceptical they said nothing.

As the quiet settled again John Lane thoughtlessly sought to put an arm under his head. The pain cut like a knife. He lowered the arm, saw the handsome woman watching him, and sighed. He wasn't sure a man other than her late husband would be able to live with her masculinity. But she was handsome, no doubt about that. Not pretty as a girl might have been, but handsome the way unisex people often were.

It turned cold which meant the night was well advanced. Marshal Holt refused to let Bob Lytle go stoke the stove. His lapses earlier when he had allowed his hostages some leniency evidently no longer obtained.

Evelyn sat like a statue, features stubbornly set, mood unchanged since they'd been at the barn. Her rider was sitting on the floor, dozing from time to time. What brought him wide awake was the same sound that startled the others. The racket dispelled the notion that there was only one man out there.

Two gunshots so close together they could almost have been made simultaneously. After that silence, Bob Lytle broke it with one of his dry remarks. 'I reckon that settles it. There's at least two of 'em.'

John Lane's interpretation of the gunfire went beyond the number of men involved. Friends did not shoot at friends. He had a suspicion but kept it to himself.

Marshal Holt rubbed a scratchy jaw as he speculated, and came up with a likely explanation. 'Somebody come up onto that feller who's been worryin' us. All things considered, I expect it was maybe Jeff or Billy.'

His hostages remained silent; this possibility could have nothing to cheer them regardless of the other man, the one who had been playing cat and mouse with them, although they were entitled to wonder who had been shot, or whether in darkness anyone had.

Their wonderment was ended when a voice called strongly. 'Marshal, you in there?'

Holt looked so relieved he almost smiled as he called back. 'Yeah. Did you get that son of a bitch?'

Instead of answering the question the same dour-sounding voice called again. 'Me'n Billy are comin' over ... All right?'

'Come ahead,' Holt called back, and started for the door, then halted, pondered briefly and jerked his head for Bob Lytle to walk ahead of him up the hall, through the parlour to the front door.

Lytle did not hesitate but as he passed his employer, he softly said, 'From the fry pan into the fire.'

Evelyn Scott and John Lane listened, heard the front door open and a quick exchange of indistinguishable words indicated that Marshal Holt had been joined by the tall, unpleasant man and his stocky nephew.

Evelyn and John strained to hear, but the speakers were distant and seemed not to be speaking very loudly. The woman said, 'I'd hoped Ben would have settled those two.'

John said nothing because three sets of footfalls

were approaching. Everett Holt was the first through
the door, he was beaming. Behind him, hatless and
dishevelled, came the taciturn tall man and his
nephew. Part of their story was explainable by their
appearance. Their clothes were filthy, only the older
man had a holstered weapon, and without doubt they
had been walking instead of riding. The tall man
looked more sour than usual.

Marshal Holt was expansive but his companions
sought places to sit. They looked tired, whisker
stubbled and gaunt.

'He caught 'em,' the lawman stated. 'I figured it
had to be something like that when they didn't come
back. ... Caught 'em, turned their horses loose an' left
'em tied to some trees.'

Lytle cocked an eyebrow. 'Who caught them?'

Marshal Holt's redeemed good nature did not
extend to the man who had been needling him since
yesterday. 'Arthur Barnes, who'd you think?'

Lytle, for once did not say what he was thinking.
Evelyn sat stone-facedly regarding the men who had
escaped. Her only comment was: 'Killers don't take
prisoners.'

'This one did,' growled the unpleasant tall man.

'Then how did you get the gun?'

'We come into the barn on foot without makin' no
noise. There was a feller in there with his back to us,
havin' a smoke as he watched the house. Billy come
up behind him, grabbed him around the neck. In the
scuffle his gun fell out of its holster. Before I could
reach them the feller worked around and hit Billy,
knocked him down. I got hold of the gun. It's
darker'n the inside of a boot in that barn ... The feller
ducked outside somewhere. I tried a sound-shot but
couldn't see him.'

Lytle said, 'So whoever he is got away.'

The lawman and his friends put unfriendly gazes on the rangeman. None of them answered him. John Lane and the handsome woman exchanged a glance. John was wondering whether the mysterious stranger had been hit. If he had, he'd be out of it. If he hadn't, and was actually as cold-blooded as he had appeared to be, John would have bet new money he was still out there somewhere, and that made the situation different. None of the men in the room excepting Bob Lytle and himself could risk leaving the house.

Jeff jerked his head at Billy. they walked out of the room to search for the kitchen, it had been a very long and arduous day without anything to eat for both of them.

Marshal Holt sat down. He still looked dog-tired and soiled, but the near-hopeless expression no longer showed. Evidence that he was back to normal was what he said to the handsome woman. 'Ma'm, I been settin' in here all night admirin' you. Widow-women can't make it on their own in this kind of country.'

Her response even shocked John Lane. 'You blundering idiot, I've already made it. When you're dust I'll still be making it. If you're an example of what government lawmen are, then it's no wonder we have renegades and bandits all over the territory.'

Marshal Holt rocked a little as he sat giving the woman hostile look for look. He seemed to be searching for an appropriate answer when Jeff and Billy returned from raiding the kitchen. They didn't look any better but they probably felt better.

Billy built and fired up a smoke. The smell was an improvement over the musty smell which was still evident. He too admired the handsome woman.

Through a lazy upward drift of smoke he said, 'You been a widow for some time, ma'm?'

Evelyn withered him with a look and said nothing. The reproof rolled off Billy like water off a duck. He said, 'I was thinkin', ma'm, I been a long time without no sleep an' you'n me could ....'

Marshal Holt interrupted. 'Boy, you ain't in no town dancehall. Jeff, didn't you learn him better manners'n to talk to a lady like that?'

The dour man ignored his nephew and considered Marshal Holt from beneath beetling brows. 'Everett, leave off the lad. Him an' me let you talk us into this damned job. You said there'd be nothin' to it, just ride up in here, surprise the outlaw and take him back with us ... Well, I can tell you Barnes could have shot us an' didn't, an' we been walkin' since well before midnight ... Nothin' to it, eh?'

Everett Holt bristled. 'Jeff, you done this before with me, we both know things don't always go the way they're supposed to.'

'Everett,' the unpleasant man said gruffly. 'That warn't Barnes we snuck up on in the barn ... you know who that was?'

Marshal Holt sat gazing at the disgruntled man without replying. John Lane, watching them both and listening, began to suspect the marshal either knew who had been worrying them or had a pretty good idea who it might be.

'You already told me at the door,' Holt said, 'Now leave it lie.'

Jeff nodded slightly. 'I'm willing to, but if I didn't hit him. I ain't sure *he'll* leave it lie.'

Lane and the rangerider exchanged a look. It *was* someone out of the marshal's past. Billy stubbed out his smoke and settled himself against the wall eyeing

Evelyn Scott. She ignored him.

The chill became particularly noticeable. Marshal Holt sent Billy to fire up the stove. After his nephew was gone Jeff said, 'Everett, Barnes ain't no one's fool. He took a game trail through some rocks, come out behind us slick as you please.'

Holt asked what Barnes had said. Jeff slouched and wagged his head. 'He lost the wolf an' was comin' back through some trees when he heard the dog bark. He said strangers come up in here once, maybe twice a year. When that's happened before he sort of hung back until he got a look at them.'

'He seen us?' the lawman asked.

'He knew our horses, seen 'em as he was ridin' back, slid back into the trees, an' I just told you the rest of it.'

Marshal Holt made a mistake. 'You let him get behind you? That's what schoolboys do.'

True or not it was a tactless thing to say, especially to a man who had walked most of the night to get back, had blisters to prove it, hadn't had a decent meal all day, and by nature was just naturally unpleasant.

Jeff arose slowly to his feet. 'Everett, there ain't goin' to be no bounty money this time.'

'Yes there will be,' the marshal exclaimed. 'He's still out there. You didn't hear no horse leavin' did you?'

Jeff stared, so did the others. 'Are you losin' your mind?' Jeff asked. 'I wasn't talkin' about him in the barn, I was talkin' about Barnes. He left us tied more'n eight hours ago. We'll never find him again until maybe next fall an' me'n Billy got work to do at home.'

Marshal Holt put his head slightly to one side before speaking again. 'All right. If that's the way you want it, go on home. I'll stay after Barnes like I been doin'.'

'For all it's got you is this here mess.'

Marshal Holt gestured. 'Go, take a couple of horses an' ride for home.'

Billy appeared in the doorway. 'There's somethin' goin' on outside.'

His uncle turned on him. 'Well – what is it?'

The stocky younger man shook his head. 'I seen a light, looked like a long way off comin' in this direction from the north.'

Jeff faced the handsome woman. 'How close are your neighbours?'

'Four, five miles – *south*.'

Jeff and Marshal Holt turned back to the stocky younger man who still had a bruise showing from John Lane's punch. The lawman gestured, 'Go see, Billy.'

His uncle countered the order. 'Stay right where you are,' he told his nephew. 'Everett,' the tall man growled. 'If you want to know go yourself ... I don't think neither me nor Billy winged that feller. Go ahead, walk out front and look around.'

Marshal Holt regarded his companions dispassionately. 'First little sign of trouble an' you two want to run for it.'

The dour man looked at his nephew. 'Go look out from the parlour, Billy, but don't go outside.'

As the stocky younger man departed Evelyn Scott, silent for the last few minutes, and addressed the unpleasant man. 'Who was the man in the barn?'

Holt spoke swiftly. 'It don't concern you, Miz Scott. You got a lot more to worry about than somethin' that don't concern you.'

Jeff, looking disgusted, left the bedroom to join his

nephew in the parlour. There was no light, possibly there never had been. Billy was tired enough to imagine things. Jeff cuffed the lad lightly on the shoulder as he said, 'Soon's we can, Billy, we're headin' for home.'

Billy stared, 'What about the bounty money?'

'Barnes is fifty miles away by now, Billy, an' by the time we pick up his trail and start after him he'll be maybe another forty, fifty miles on his way. If the marshal wants to keep after him, fine, but he's gettin' paid an' we ain't.'

Jeff went to the kitchen which had barely enough pre-dawn light to aid visibility, and ate as he stuffed a croaker sack with more food. He also appropriated a bottle of whiskey.

Billy kept his vigil in the parlour stubbornly unwilling to admit the light he had seen could have been an illusion, or maybe a star down the horizon. He now made the worst mistake of his life, he went over to the door to get a better look at the sky, a gun roared, Billy was knocked half way across the parlour, and when his uncle came rushing from the kitchen Billy looked up to smile slightly as he said, 'Tell Ma an' Paw goodbye for me.'

By the time Marshal Holt and Evelyn Scott got out there, Billy was dead.

Jeff sprang up white-faced and started for the door. Evelyn stopped him. 'Do you want to get killed too?'

The tall man stopped with his back to them, stood a long time like that before very slowly turning back. The slug had hit Billy higher than the one that had hit John Lane, but nothing had impeded its progress. It went through his soft parts and was found years later embedded in some fireplace mortar.

Marshal Holt did as he'd done when John Lane had been shot. He stood looking down and sucking his teeth, showing no concern and probably feeling none, until he raised his eyes. The tall, unpleasant man was staring steadily at the marshal as his words fell like lead. 'Nothin' to it, you said. Like fallin' off a log. Ride in up here, find him, tie him an' take him back … well, there lies easy as fallin' off a log, Everett.'

There was nothing for the lawman to say, and he wisely remained silent.

'What do I tell his folks? That you told him to go keep watch and he run into a bullet?'

Marshal Holt moved to a chair and sank down. He remained like that even after the others had carried Billy's body to the back of the house and left it on a steel cot in a large storeroom.

As they were leaving the little room Jeff addressed Evelyn Scott. 'Lady, if I was you I'd make your peace with that feller out there. I don't think we hit him. Lady, his name's Max Hyde, if he can't get at Everett inside the house he'll burn it down an' kill you all. Max Hyde's got a demon ridin' him. He'd walk through a field of bullets to get one shot at Everett Holt. Take my advice, call out to him, tell him who you are, that you never seen Everett Holt before he rode into your yard … I don't know, Max Hyde's as deadly as they come, but you got nothin' to lose. Try talkin' to him.'

'How about you?'

'I can't leave Billy behind. I'll have to stay.'

'Does Hyde know you too?'

'Well yes, he knows me'n Billy, only we had nothin' to do with what happened to Hyde's family. We wasn't even in the country at the time. … He's kill-crazy, ma'm. It just might not make any difference that you didn't know the marshal ... Hyde's got reason to feel like he does.'

Jeff nodded and walked past back into the parlour where Everett Holt was still sitting slumped.

Evelyn came a few steps later. Jeff was standing regarding the lawman. Evelyn passed down the hall to the bedroom and told John Lane what had happened, who had done it, and what Jeff had said to her.

NINE
Daybreak

Evelyn went to the kitchen to make coffee. She was accompanied by the federal lawman. Jeff sat broodingly uncommunicative in the bedroom with John Lane. Each attempt Lane made to start a conversation was received in frozen silence.

If the killer was still around he did not make his presence known. Dawn was coming, a long, frightening night would shortly end. Evelyn ignored the marshal leaning in the doorway admiring her. She'd had one chance to be alone in the kitchen hours earlier after the first shooting. She had thought Marshal Holt would allow her to make coffee without being watched. She was wrong.

There was an old dragoon revolver in one of the kitchen drawers loaded and ready. It had belonged to her late husband's father. It hadn't been touched in fifteen years, but she knew it could be fired. What she was less certain about was whether she could kill a man.

As she worked, busy with her private thoughts, Marshal Holt asked several innocuous questions such as who had founded the ranch, how she had met her husband, and when she told him how that had happened the marshal raised an eyebrow. 'Your folks homesteaded in this country? Where was your paw from?'

'Indiana, where there is deep, rich soil. It was a common mistake.'

Holt nodded understandingly, about a third of the wanted men he had run down had been destitute settlers whose choice was to watch their broods starve or steal money so they wouldn't starve.

He softly said, 'Lady, everythin' west of the Missouri River is hard country. You know the saying: Hard on men but a living hell for women an' horses.'

Evelyn might have encouraged this discussion under different circumstances; she had watched her parents break their hearts on Tandy Meadow, she had felt their pain, had seen their discouragement, had wonderful memories of them and how they had tried to hide failure from their little girl.

She did volunteer a little, in an off-hand way, as though she were talking to herself. 'They're buried near the log house. They died the year after I married my husband.'

'Lady, it ain't a country for women, greenhorns or outlaws, an' as time passes it'll get even harder for them kind.'

She turned to look directly at him. 'Who is Max Hyde?'

A tinge of faint colour came into his beard-stubbled face. 'Jeff! Him an' his flannel mouth. What did he tell you?'

'That Max Hyde has reason to kill you.'

'Did he now. Well, Jeff was off on a drive when me'n Hyde had a run-in. All he knows is hearsay, an' if you don't know it, you'd ought to: Folks talk, make up stories, figure out some real fine lies ... Jeff's got trouble with his tongue.'

She answered that from personal observation. 'It'd seemed to me he doesn't talk much.'

'He did this time, didn't he?'

'I don't know, Marshal.'

'He wasn't there, he don't know what happened ... Lady, that coffee water's boiling.'

She got cold meat and potatoes from the cooler, sliced coarse dark bread and set three places at the table. Holt watched her every move. When she finished at the stove and piled food on a platter she said, 'You can fetch your friend, Marshal.'

He nodded and started to turn away. Evelyn was standing beside a drawer waiting and watching. He may have had one of those intuitive flashes. More likely, having been at his profession so many years, instinct warned him often, and usually well. He stood looking at her. She had one hand above the drawer knob.

He crossed the room, shoved her aside and opened the drawer. For a moment he stood regarding the big old pistol before lifting it, hefting it and examining it for loads. As he looked at her said, 'Lady, that damned old gun would most likely explode in your face.'

He shucked the old weapon empty and dropped it back into the drawer which he closed as he said, 'You better come along with me.'

He herded her to the back bedroom. Only John Lane was there. Holt's brow wrinkled. 'Where's Jeff?' he asked. The man in the bed jerked a thumb in the direction of the storeroom.

Evelyn went to her chair, sat down and gazed at the hands in her lap. Billy probably had been dangerous. He just hadn't lived long enough for her to make that judgement.

When Jeff returned to the bedroom he put a
sulphurous look upon Marshal Holt, who told him
food was waiting in the kitchen. The unpleasant
man's retort was short. 'Go eat it. Me, I don't have no
appetite.'

Marshal Holt studied the tall, sour man. 'Keep an
eye on this one,' he told the tall man and jerked his
head for Evelyn to precede him toward the kitchen.

John Lane waited until they were gone and the
unpleasant man was sitting slouched before trying
once more to get a conversation going.

'How long's Hyde goin' to keep this up?' He asked,
and got a baleful look from the tall man. 'Until he's
damned well finished what he come here for ... I'd
guess he's been shaggin' Everett Holt about for over a
year now.'

'Then why did you and Billy ride with the
marshal?'

'We heard two stories. One was that Max had got
shot an' killed over a poker game in New Messico.
The other story was that he'd taken the steam trains
to go back where they come from to forget.' Jeff's
humourless gaze showed irony. 'I guess them stories
was made up. T'tell you the truth I was always a mite
doubtful. I knew Max Hyde pretty well. I told Everett
Max would drop dead before he'd give up huntin'
him.'

'He didn't believe you?'

Jeff straightened a little in the chair. He had looked
bad when he had emerged out of the night after an
eight-mile hike, but with the killing of his nephew he
looked worse. 'He said where we was goin' Max Hyde
would never even come close.'

John Lane was quiet for a while, but the unpleasant
man had started talking and continued to do so with

scorch in every sentence. 'I rode with Everett Holt lots of times. We racked up a good score of captures, split the money, an' I got to tell you it was a heap better'n I ever made farming or runnin' cattle … But like my wife told me this last time me'n Billy rode to meet the marshal, a man's luck lasts just so long and the hell of it is, he don't know when it leaves him … He finds out like we found out on this ride with the marshal.'

'Tell me about Max Hyde, Jeff.'

The unpleasant man sat in brooding silence. Whether he hadn't heard the question or, more likely, the pain of loss and the message he had to carry back with him, wherever home was, had borne down harder on his spirit, John Lane was never to know.

Evelyn Scott and the federal lawman returned from the kitchen. She sought a chair, sat and raised her eyes at the rangeman across the room, silent and motionless. He had been fascinated by the conversation between John Lane and the unpleasant man.

He shrugged indifferently at her un-asked question about breakfast. Like most of his kind, Bob Lytle could go for long periods without eating. It went with his line of work. Sometimes kitchens were fifteen miles away, especially during the riding season.

The stove required stoking. This time when someone left the room to take care of this chore, Marshal Holt walked behind him.

When they were in the kitchen by the wood box Lytle reached for a scantling with his back to the marshal as he said, 'The way I got this figured, Mister Holt, even if it was still dark an' you could get your horse, that feller'd be waitin' for you. Now, it bein' daylight an' all,' Lytle stopped speaking long enough to load the firebox of the stove. He saw the coffee pot, hefted it, filled a previously used cup before saying the rest of it. 'You got about as much chance as a snowball in hell.'

Holt leaned in the doorway as he'd done earlier, only this time there was no admiration in his gaze. 'You been annoyin' me all night, Mister Lytle.'

The rangeman emptied the cup, re-filled it and offered it to the older man. Holt ignored the offer. 'As near as I can see, Marshal, there's no way you're goin' to ride away from here – unless you find Mister Hyde first.'

'I'll wait out the son of a bitch,' the lawman retorted. 'Max Hyde ain't very smart. I got food an' hostages in here, all he's got is hay in the barn and suckin' air for food. I know him, cowboy. I've known him since he come into the territory. Worthless little idiotic damn fool.'

Lytle came back with one of his needling comments. 'There aren't no brains required to aim and shoot, Marshal. You ought to know that, bein' in your line of work an' all. It only takes fair vision, a target an' a steady trigger-finger … what did you do to get this feller on your trail like a wolf?'

Marshal Holt jerked his head as he stepped clear of the doorway. Bob Lytle trooped back to the bedroom. It would be a while before that part of the house got warm.

They were sitting in long silence when a man called from out in the newday brilliance. 'Marshal? You hear me? You're bottled up in there. I'm goin' to do to you what you done to my family … Unless you walk out of there alone. I know you Jeff'n Billy in there. I figure Billy's hurt bad enough to be helpless … You hear me, Marshal?'

In the bedroom they all looked at Everett Holt, who

was leaning against the wall. He acted as though he had heard nothing. Jeff broke the silence. 'I told you, Everett ... I told the lady here he'll burn the house down with us inside it.'

Marshal Holt scoffed. 'How's he goin' to sneak up here an' do that, Jeff, if you're in the parlour watching?'

The unpleasant man had the answer, 'Same way it was done before – get around behind the house. The difference is that this time it won't be dark.'

Marshal Holt straightened off the wall. To John Lane he looked very troubled. 'Jeff, you keep these folks quiet. I'm goin' to try something. He wants it man to man, I'll see what can be arranged.'

After the lawman left the room John Lane and Bob Lytle exchanged a look. Evelyn told them about her father-in-law's old horse pistol. She seemed to blame herself. Lytle shook his head at her. 'Wasn't your fault, ma'm. He expects things like that an' you got no experience.'

Jeff arose and went to stand in the doorway. There was not a sound. He lingered for a few minutes then returned to this chair as he wagged his head. 'Don't get too hopeful. That old devil knows more ways to skin a cat than you can shake a stick at.'

Again Lytle made a tart comment. 'But a cat ain't armed.'

Jeff ignored Lytle, shoved out long legs to cross them at the ankles and return to his earlier brooding state.

The handsome woman asked John Lane how he felt. He answered in one word. 'Hungry.'

Evelyn looked enquiringly at Jeff. He seemed not to have heard their exchange, his gaze was fixed on the scuffed toes of his old boots. He only roused himself when Evelyn asked if she could return to the kitchen for some food for the wounded man.

Jeff dourly shook his head and went back to his reverie.

Someone hurled another rock at the front of the house. The hostages and their guard, roused by the racket, waited for whatever came next. It was a short wait, there were still echoes when two gunshots made their ears ring.

The stone had come from the front of the house. Not enough time elapsed between the stone-throwing and the gunshots for both to have been accomplished by the same man.

No one spoke, but Jeff arose, leaned in the doorway, returned to his chair but now he sat on the edge of it, no longer losing himself in his thoughts.

'Two,' he murmured.

Lytle said, 'Maybe Ben teamed up with Hyde.'

'His name ain't Ben, it's Arthur Barnes,' Jeff exclaimed.

Unruffled Bob Lytle then said, 'Barnes.'

Jeff shook his head. 'Didn't you hear that runnin' horse last night?'

'Mister I heard *two* runnin' horses last night. One was your horse the other one was the marshal's horse.'

Jeff raised cold eyes to the cowboy, but what Lytle had said hit him between the eyes. He arose to go find the marshal. From the doorway he warned that any movement, any noise of any kind and he would come back to kill them all.

They listened to his diminishing footfalls. Bob Lytle grinned from ear to ear. 'That rattled him.'

No one agreed or disagreed, they were listening intently.

There was not a sound except for the faintly-heard

bawling of a cow. Lytle, the lifelong rangeman spoke absently about that. 'Some calf filled his belly with milk an' went off into the shade to sleep. His mammy can bawl until she's hoarse, them little calves is as arbitrary as they come.'

Lytle was silent for a while. The next time he spoke it was concerning something that had been troubling him since yesterday. He mentioned it now in the manner of an individual trying to sort something out by putting it into words.

'You remember when Ben come up lookin' for work, Miz Scott?'

She remembered, she also had been wondering about the same thing. 'I remember. My husband said many times that no man can keep his private life private for very long with other men … My guess is that if Ben killed a man there was a reason other than just to shoot someone.'

Lytle hadn't been thinking exactly the same thing. 'We set under many a tree talkin' about things. There wasn't nothin' personal ever brought up, but I'm havin' a real hard time thinking of Ben as a murderer.'

John Lane entered the discussion with a suggestion. 'Jeff might know the details. It'd be useless to ask the marshal.'

Jeff returned to the room, swung his chair to face the door and sat down. He completely ignored the hostages until John asked where the marshal was, then Jeff turned and spoke. 'I couldn't find the old devil. I'll tell you one thing for a blessed fact, he can be slippery'n an eel.'

Lytle shrugged. 'Bein' slippery ain't goin' to be enough, friend. He needs steel plate under his shirt an' the luck of the Irish.'

Jeff returned his vigil to the doorway, he only made one more comment about the federal officer. 'If he can't ferret them out, no one can.'

Again Lytle made a practical remark. 'It ain't him findin' them, friend. It's them findin' him. All they got to do is get comfortable an' wait. With no one likely to ride by, neighbours or the like, they can set out there for weeks.'

'Without food?' Evelyn asked.

Her rider nodded his head. 'Ma'm, there's enough grub in the bunkhouse ... an' there's somethin' else. There is two of them, not one of them. Want me to guess about the second one?'

The woman shook her head. She too had had time to speculate. She no more believed the man she knew as Ben Tuttle had run for it than she believed the sky could fall.

What bothered them all as time passed, was the silence. Jeff was restless, as he had every right to be; if Marshal Holt escaped, only Jeff would be left, a not very pleasant prospect.

He prowled the house with a sixgun in his fist, much more concerned with the missing lawman than he was in a killer waiting outside.

John Lane swung his feet to the floor. Evelyn sprang up to push him back on the bed. 'I don't have enough worries,' she scolded. 'Get back under those covers. Don't add to the other things I worry about ... Bob? If he tries that again, punch him.'

Lytle looked shocked. 'Hit a wounded man?'

'Then I'll do it. Mister Lane, lie back down. Go to sleep.'

Lytle had not been sleeping, nor had he liked her suggestion. He reddened but held his tongue. He had in his time worked for dozens of cowmen, some he had not liked, others were absentee stockmen with overbearing manager-rangebosses. He had no complaints about working for a female-woman the last four or five years, but he had only rarely thought of Evelyn Scott as a woman. Maybe a time or two when she had ridden with him and Ben, had stood against the wind, then she put him in mind of a woman, but the moment the wind died and she called for either Ben or him to do something, she was an employer, a boss, one that thought and talked pretty much like her husband had sounded.

Both of her riders had often discussed Evelyn Scott since the passing of her husband. They had come to an identical conclusion: She was handsome, she had a nice build, she looked good on a horse, the only things lacking were a beard and squinty eyes for Evelyn Scott to be a spitting image of a lot of men they had known.

They admired her, approved of most of her judgements, but good-looking or not, she simply did not fit their idea of what a woman should be, and that must have constituted quite a drawback in Evelyn Scott because neither of her riders had been near a town in six months.

TEN
Nothing Goes On Forever

Jeff was leaning gloomily in the doorway looking from one hostage to the other, evidently weighing some personal notion about them, when a man laughed loudly. This noise was followed by a gunshot. Bob Lytle waited out the last echo before drily saying, 'That darned fool went outside.'

He alluded to the federal marshal; none of the others thought differently. Jeff lingered in the doorway balefully regarding the others before he raised and cocked his sixgun as he warned them not to move, not to even think about leaving the room, then he faded from sight.

Lytle made another dry comment. 'There's some mighty poor shots out there.'

Maybe, but right now none of the hostages knew whether anyone had been shot outside the house or not.

A loud, rough voice called from the yard. 'Marshal! You ain't goin' nowhere. You ain't goin' out of this yard except to get buried.'

Lane and Lytle exchanged a look. Evidently whoever had fired had not hit the marshal. If they had thought otherwise there wouldn't have been a taunting call.

Evelyn arose, paced twice the width of the room and halted near the door as Jeff abruptly appeared. They were less than five feet apart when he raised a stiff finger, poked her hard in the chest and said, 'I told you not to move.'

She returned to the chair, still exasperated. 'Where is the marshal?' she asked, and got a dolorous wag of the head from Jeff. 'I'll tell you one thing – he ain't in the house.'

They had already arrived at that conclusion. John Lane felt no admiration for Everett Holt, but right now he grudgingly respected his courage. There were two men out there who would kill him on sight. Two to one odds any time left something to be desired, but when a man's life was on the line, two to one odds were intolerable.

The wait began again, the sun was rising, the house was chilly because the stove had burned down, but most of all the waiting, the lack of real knowledge concerning what might – and probably could – happen, was wearing them all down. For the unpleasant man named Jeff, this seemingly endless cat and mouse game was made inexorably demoralising; his nephew was growing cold in the storeroom.

Warmth came gradually into the house, unnoticed by its inhabitants, particularly since the stone-thrower hurled another rock against the house, its abrupt silence-shattering sound making nerves crawl.

Bob Lytle, the laconic rangeman who had seemed the least affected, stood up, hitched at his shellbelt with its empty holster and announced he'd had enough, and walked out into the hallway. The handsome woman and John Lane held their breath.

Within what seemed only seconds, a gunshot sounded from inside the house. Evelyn Scott sprang up and ran to the doorway. She stopped dead still. John Lane moved to throw off his blankets, something she normally would have swiftly reacted to except that now her body was rigid at something she was watching in the hallway.

John Lane reached the doorway, which she was blocking, shouldered her aside and leaned to look past.

Sunlight did not reach into the hallway but there was sufficient light to see by. Two men were locked in a fierce struggle on the floor. One was Bob Lytle, the other was the unpleasant man.

Lytle was holding the other man's gun wrist with both hands which prevented him from warding off the savage pummelling he was getting from Jeff. Most of those blows either missed or grazed Lytle. Jeff's right hand would normally be the one he would use in this kind of a struggle. But he was nevertheless doing damage.

John Lane shoved the woman aside, took three long steps, saw Jeff's eyes suddenly look up, swung as hard as he could and Jeff's hat sailed out into the parlour as his head snapped back seconds before his body turned limp.

John Lane helped Lytle to his feet. His face was splotchy from blows, there was a thin red trickle where one blow had split his lip.

He came upright with Jeff's gun in his fist. When Lane asked if he was all right, the laconic cowboy replied while gazing down at the unconscious man. He laconically said, 'Good thing you come along, I'd have killed the son of a bitch.'

Another time John Lane might have laughed, right

now he knelt to roll Jeff onto his back. The blow had
caught the unpleasant man squarely on the point of
the jaw. He had no blood showing but it would be
quite a spell before he'd remember his own name.

Evelyn started to say something; her cowboy turned
and very candidly said, 'Ma'm, shut up! Just keep
quiet.'

She obeyed, lingered in the doorway as John Lane
got to his feet, a little unsteadily, leaned against the
wall briefly before saying they needed some rope to
tie the unconscious man. Evelyn left the doorway,
squeezed around the men, went to the kitchen and
returned with a coil of cotton clothesline. They
secured Jeff at the ankles and with both wrists lashed
behind his back. As they were doing this Bob Lytle
drily said, 'Well now, Mister Lane, seems the boot
might be on the other foot. At least for now.'

John Lane looked at the handsome woman. 'I need
a gun,' he said. She surprised both men by going to
the storeroom and returning with the sixgun Billy
had worn. She handed it to Lane without a word.

The gun had one empty casing, otherwise it was
lethal. Lane went back to get his boots, other effects
including his shellbelt and returned with a sixgun in
the holster.

He took a leaf from Bob Lytle's book. He did not
ask the handsome woman to stay in the bedroom, he
told her to do it but at least he explained why. There
were no windows in the bedroom, there was only the
door which led into the gloomy hallway. It was
probably as safe a place they could leave her.

After Lytle and Lane slipped ahead into the
parlour, Evelyn Scott pushed and rolled until she had
the unconscious man inside the bedroom. She left
him partially blocking the door.   What she did after

that would have surprised both Lytle and Lane, she rummaged in a dresser, flung aside bits of clothing, a sachet of rose petals, a thick blanket and came up holding a small nickel-plated five shot revolver, a gift from her late husband years earlier. She had only fired the little gun once, at a mountain lion crouching to attack. The slug had gone through the cat's neck making him fall, get up and run.

She never used the little gun again. When she had reason to ride armed it was with a standard Colt in her holster. If she had hit that cougar in the neck with a forty-five slug he wouldn't have run ten feet before dropping dead.

Her husband had once told her the little gun would only protect her at very close range. The cougar hadn't been more than thirty feet distant. Maybe her husband had meant *very* close range, five or ten feet.

She put the little gun in a pocket of her riding skirt where it scarcely showed, stood a while in thought then left the room she'd been told to stay in, edged around Jeff and went on tip-toes to the entryway into the parlour.

There was no sign of Lytle or Lane. Her intention was to get close enough across the parlour to be able to see into the yard.

She got half way toward the window when a gunshot sounded. Glass blew inward all around her. She winced and moved away from the front wall.

A second gunshot sounded, this one seeming to come from somewhere over on the west side of the house. The handsome woman retreated back to the hallway where Jeff was conscious and feebly straining against his bonds. She stepped over him, he looked up and said, 'Where are they?'

'Who?'

'I heard the window break. Where are them fellers outside?'

Her reply was tart. 'I don't know and don't particularly care. Mister Lane and my rider are gone.'

'You mean outside the house?'

'I don't know.'

Jeff flopped until he could prop himself in the doorway before speaking again. 'I'd admire a sip of the barleycorn, ma'm. Mister Lane hits like a kickin' mule.'

She ignored him to listen, but as before there was nothing to be heard, evidently the deadly manhunt was being enacted somewhere beyond the house. She knew how good at this sort of thing Marshal Holt was. She was much less sure about her rangeman and John Lane, another rangeman.

Jeff abruptly spoke. 'It's away from the house anyway. They'll meet yonder somewhere ... I expect Marshal Holt thinks Lane an' your rider are still in here ... What I doubt he knows is that the odds against him are now four to one. Miz Scott, did you ever hear of anyone walkin' away from them kind of odds?'

Instead of replying she got the bottle John Lane had been succoured by, took it over and when the unpleasant man opened his mouth and tipped his head back, she poured, took back the bottle and returned to her chair.

Jeff eyed her through moments when colour came into his cheeks and his normally dull, cynical eyes noticeably brightened.

He said, 'Lady, I'm goin' to tell you what happened. Everett Holt'n couple other families of us all lived fairly close. There was a homesteader come in an' took up land. He didn't bother no one the first year, but the second year he got hold of some cattle somewhere an' run them over land the rest of us had been grazing over for about ten years.

'Couple of the neighbours rode over to explain how things was to him. He was a kind of peppery feller, not very tall but wiry and tough. He run them off with a shotgun ...

'We had another meetin' after that. Everett said for the rest of us to stay home and never mind he'd take care of things. ...Which he did. He waited until the clodhopper'n his wife and little kids was fast asleep, poured coal oil everywhere and set the house afire.'

Evelyn was staring. 'Hyde ...?'

'Yes'm. He was the only one come out alive. He didn't get home until there was nothing but red coals and ash ... I don't know how he knew it was Everett, but I guess that wouldn't be hard to figure out.'

'How long ago was that?' The handsome woman asked.

'Four years ago come next autumn.'

'... His whole family ...?'

'Yes'm, his woman, their two children – a little boy about six an' a little girl about four.'

Evelyn settled deeper into her chair. 'What kind of a man would burn children to death?'

Jeff did not respond. The liquor was warming him, encouraging him to think back. He only said one more thing. 'Money, ma'm. Money's all that got me'n Billy ridin' with Everett. We hadn't had a decent crop in three, four years, an' mostly hunting men down and catching them off-guard worked real good ... Just not this time.'

Evelyn arose to pace the room. When Jeff asked for another couple of swallows from the bottle she ignored him, removed the little nickel-plated revolver from her pocket and the man said, 'You had that thing all the time?' She ignored the question as she crossed to the door, ready to step over him when he spoke again. 'Leave it be, Miz Scott. Everett's damned good, but not *this* good. There's four of 'em after his hide ... They'll get him, mark my word. If you go out there you could get shot, at the very least you could make them fellers who want Everett to take their minds off their work ... Just set down an' wait. It won't be long now, what with daylight and all.'

It was good advice but the handsome woman didn't take it. She stepped over the man's legs and went cautiously up the hall. The last time she'd entered the parlour there had been a gunshot, probably by some watcher who could distinguish movement in the parlour without determining much else.

So far there had been a fair amount of gunfire, but except for John Lane and Billy, no particular injuries.

She stayed clear of the window as she worked her way across the parlour's south wall, past the huge old stone hearth to the opposite wing of the house. There, she found an open window which had not been opened in several years. Hair stood up at the back of her neck. Someone had either got inside, intended to get inside or had planned on doing it and had changed his mind.

She was not tempted to poke her head out to look around. She was hesitating in the doorway when a man's voice very quietly spoke to her.

'Who are you?' The question was followed by the sound of a gun being cocked.

Her answer was crisp, despite having been startled. 'Evelyn Scott. Who are you?'

He didn't answer the question. 'I figured it would be you. Barnes said you'd be inside with the others.'

She turned slowly, not out of any particular interest in the stranger but at what he had said: Barnes. She sighed to herself. Marshal Holt had been correct, Ben Tuttle, her hired rider, was Arthur Barnes, a fugitive wanted for murder. She asked where Barnes was. The man opposite her with the steady gun was lithe, wiry, not tall but the kind of an individual who rarely tired, never abandoned an objective, and right now looked as though he hadn't been near a barber in ages, hadn't shaved very recently either, and was as gaunt, and sunken-eyed as a man whose sole, driving motivation had allowed him no rest for a very long time. He did not tell her his name but she knew what it would be: Max Hyde.

He did not lower the gun. It was cocked and its ugly snout never wavered from the middle of her chest. 'Where's Jeff?'

'Disarmed and tied at the other end of the house.'

The wiry older man gestured with his weapon. 'Show me.'

She led off without a qualm. Hyde had not been hostile, he had been matter-of-fact, which was something she had always appreciated in folks.

She entered the hallway, stepped aside so Jeff and the wiry man could look at each other, which they did without a sound passing between them before Max Hyde raised his sixgun and fired from a distance of less than ten feet.

Evelyn's hand instinctively flew to her mouth. She couldn't have moved or made a sound if her soul had depended on it.

Jeff's head bounced off the door jamb before falling forward on his chest. There was a brief showing of blood in the exact centre of his shirt, but that was all.

The wiry man said, 'He had it coming. Now let's get

back to the other side of the house, there's still another couple of them.'

She moved as though in a trance, completely overlooking what he had said about there being a couple of them. Only when they had returned to the bedroom with the open window and he asked where Billy was, did it occur to her that he did not know, so she told him.

'He's in the storeroom, dead.'

The cold-eyed lithe man seemed about to march her to the other end of the house to verify what she had said. He may have had that in mind but a flurry of gunshots outside made him pull up very straight as he listened, no longer interested in the woman.

When the firing ended Max Hyde gestured with his killer-gun. 'Peek out there, lady.'

She obeyed without thinking. Witnessing a deliberate cold-blooded murder had numbed part of her mind. When she pulled her head back Max Hyde asked what she had seen. She shook her head. 'Nothing, just a fading patch of gunsmoke somewhere in the vicinity of the bunkhouse or maybe the barn.'

'No movement? No bodies?'

'No.'

For a moment Max Hyde was thoughtfully silent before leathering his sixgun and crossing to the window. He looked out and pulled back. There was no gunshot. He said, 'Lady, stay in the house. You understand me? There's goin' to be killin' an' if you come out there you'll get shot sure as hell. No one's goin' to be gallant. Stay in here or get yourself killed.'

He dropped both legs over the sill, dropped from Evelyn's sight and was gone in an instant.

She went to a chair and sat down. She would not

have returned to the bedroom where John Lane had been lying for a fortune in gold. She would not have stepped over Jeff, the victim of a cold-blooded murder who was blocking the doorway, for anything under the sun.

There was no gunfire, silence settled and lingered. Heat increased both inside and outside. Evelyn Scott required considerable time to recover from the shock of witnessing a murder.

There began to be shadows on the east side of structures and trees. The old dog whined until she let him come inside, perhaps he could scent death because he half crossed the parlour on the way to the kitchen when he stopped dead in his tracks for a moment until she spoke, then he followed her to the kitchen where she fed him.

Outside, there was more than silence, there was an atmosphere of abandonment, as though whoever had been out there before no longer was.

Evelyn would not leave the house nor go into its east wing. She kept the big dog with her and waited for the catastrophe she felt in her bones would eventually completely engulf her.

But intuitive notions were probably more often wrong than right. This was one of those times.

ELEVEN
The Real Fugitive

When Max Hyde returned to the area of the stone trough behind the barn John Lane and Bob Lytle were waiting. Hyde said, 'He wasn't in the house.' Before he could explain the gunshot Bob Lytle gestured as he drily said, 'You wasn't very close, Mister Hyde. Look there.'

The scent of dust was noticeable but the shod-horse tracks could have been old except for that scent.

Hyde bent low, straightened around looking angry. 'You fellers let him get away?'

John replied in an identical angry tone. 'No one let him go. The son of a bitch stole my horse.'

'You didn't hear nothing?'

'Not a damned thing,' Lane explained. 'He didn't saddle up, he bridled the horse and led it out a ways so there'd be no noise.'

'Which way did he ride?'

John Lane pointed. 'South accordin' to the tracks as far as we followed them anyway.'

Max Hyde lifted out his sixgun and methodically punched out an empty casing and re-loaded the chamber from his shellbelt.

Hyde finished with the gun, holstered it and asked

why the marshal hadn't taken his own horse. The answer came from a shadowy area near the rear barn opening where the man known locally as Ben Tuttle said, 'Because I turned it loose last night an' run it off.'

Max Hyde eyed the larger, stockier man. They had met last night entirely by accident. 'Then we go after him,' Hyde stated matter-of-factly. 'We need horses, Mister Barnes.'

The Scott-rider nodded and turned back into the barn. There were two horses in stalls. He led them out to be saddled. Max Hyde went after his hidden animal and returned astride. Barnes and John Lane were mounted. There was no horse for Bob Lytle. He and Barnes spoke briefly, clasped hands and Lytle was left to watch as John Lane took the lead of the pursuers. He eventually trudged to the main-house, found the handsome woman sitting in her parlour with broken glass everywhere. When he walked in she looked up from an expressionless face. Lytle said, 'They're gone. There wasn't another horse so I stayed back. Where's Jeff?'

She rolled her head to one side without saying a word. Lytle crossed over, went down the hall and stopped. He did not move for a long time, when he eventually returned to the parlour Evelyn said, 'It was the man named Hyde. Shot him when his hands and feet were tied. Killed him without a qualm.'

Lytle went to the kitchen, got the stove going and put the coffee pot on a burner then returned to the parlour. He asked if she was all right. She nodded without looking at him. He returned to the kitchen filled one cup full of black java, filled the second one half full, went down the hall, stepped over the corpse to retrieve the bottle, went back to the kitchen to top up the second cup before taking both cups to the parlour.

Evelyn accepted the cup, clasped it in both hands for the warmth, sipped a little of it, stifled a cough, saw her rider standing with his back to her gazing out the shattered window. Without facing around he said, 'Ben was Arthur Barnes. Marshal Holt was right.'

He faced around to tell her the rest of it. 'Holt took Lane's horse and led it out a ways before mounting. Hyde, Barnes and Lane are after him.'

'Which way did he go?' She asked.

'South. He'll find the trail we use every spring to take the cattle to the meadow.' Lytle paused to empty his cup and set it aside. 'Ma'm, I got some unpleasant work to do. I can do it better with a full gut.'

She finally arose but still would not look at him as she entered the kitchen.

Lytle shook his head, wrapped the man called Jeff in one of the blankets from the bed, grunted the dead weight over a shoulder and made for the parlour, across it to the door leading to the yard. Evelyn did not look; she did not have to.

Lytle returned a quarter hour later to get Billy. He had more trouble this time. Billy was losing his death-stiffness but he was not yet entirely limp. Lytle gritted his teeth, lifted the burden and also took it down to the barn to be placed in shade.

Digging graves was nothing he, nor anyone else, enjoyed, but at least early summer had not hardened the earth. Lytle tossed tools into a wagon, went back for his meal, wondering where in hell the team horses were. Evelyn must have anticipated his thoughts because she asked if there was another saddle animal left. Lytle shook his head while eating. She left the room, left the house without Lytle knowing it, and walked briskly northwest for half an hour before she saw them standing in shade, indifferently flicking flies with their tails, dozing. She had to whistle four times before the handsome blood-bay walked toward her out of the shade.

She made a squaw-bridle, mounted the handsome horse bareback, reined off more westerly, visited three loafing areas before she found the harness horses. It was easy to cut them out and start them for home.

It was early afternoon by the time she returned to the yard where Bob Lytle had seen her coming and was leaning on the tie-rack in front of the barn when she corralled the big horses, slid off the blood-bay, led it inside to be stalled and finally came out where he eyed her thoughtfully. 'It's been a while,' he told her drily.

She leaned on the tie-rack too. 'Six or seven years, Bob. He was four when my husband gave him to me one Christmas. He's not young but neither is he old. He was always a pet.'

Lytle knew that. He and Ben had wondered why she hadn't ridden the blood-bay more. She may have anticipated that because she said, 'I just wanted him to be free, to live the way he would want to live.' She checked herself and looked a little self-consciously at him. 'You understand?'

He lied. 'Yes'm.' He did not understand but for this brief moment he saw her as a feeling human being. He had always liked her, but for this moment he felt a stir of sympathy for her, an almost instinctive wish to protect her.

He cleared his throat. It was a little late in the day for digging graves, which was an all-day job. He told her he'd head out in the morning and asked if she

wanted Billy and Jeff buried inside the ornate steel
fence where her husband, his parents and others
were buried. She shook her head and walked toward
the main-house without explaining, and that, Lytle
told himself, was the Evelyn Scott he had known for
years.

Dusk seemed to arrive early. Lytle had finished the
chores and was at the bunkhouse when she came
down to say she didn't want to eat alone. He said he'd
be along, went out back to shave and wash, even comb
his hair, before crossing the yard where a light
showed.

Evelyn had the meal prepared. She also had done a
thoughtful thing, she had strengthened his glass of
water with a taste of clear whiskey.

As they ate she mentioned John Lane. All Lytle
could say was that he liked Lane. She told him what
she knew which surprised Bob Lytle, but not for long,
at his age he knew the twists and turns life took.

They discussed the other two, both flat out under
old wagon canvas down in the barn. They were not
especially condemnatory. She told him what Jeff had
said about burning a woman and two children to
death. He paused for a moment then went back to
eating without saying a word.

She told him how Max Hyde had deliberately shot
Jeff whose arms and ankles were tied. Bob Lytle
paused to say, 'I once knew a feller who had
somethin' happen, I never knew what it was, that
turned him into a killer. It was flat out murder. He
shot three men in broad daylight in the centre of
town.'

'Did the law catch him?'

Lytle made a crooked little humourless smile.
'Them three *was* lawmen. No, as far as I know he was

never run down ... I knew him fairly well; what I've wondered since was what does a man do with his life when he's got his revenge, killed his victims; does he settle down somewhere an' take up a job? If he does, d'you expect there's a piece of his memory that'll never let him sleep decent again?'

Evelyn Scott cleared their plates away and put a large slice of apple pie in front of her rider, who was as surprised at this as he'd ever been about anything. 'You baked this, ma'm?'

She looked pleased at the implied compliment, but did not smile. 'I had to do something, Bob. Use my hands, think about something pleasant ... Is it good?'

He did not reply because his mouth was full but he rolled his eyes.

Later, when they went out front to sit under the porch overhang, she became practical again. 'I wanted John Lane to hire on as a replacement for Ben.'

'Is he goin' to?'

'I don't know. He would have let me know the day all this other business busted loose ... I'd like to have him on the ranch.'

Bob Lytle was cautious. 'Seems like a handy feller.' He looked sideways at her, but it was too dark to make out any expression, if there was any which, in her case, there usually wasn't.

He thanked her for the meal and headed for the bunkhouse. Long after his lamp had been doused the light still shone from the main-house. If Lytle had noticed he would have attributed it to her inability to sleep after having a deliberate murder committed in front of her, and perhaps her female instinct for tidiness by sweeping up broken glass and in other ways staying busy putting the main-house back in

order. He would have been wrong. She did clean up
the kitchen, but that did not take long.

She dressed warmly because even summer nights in
the high country were cold. She pocketed the little
nickel-plated revolver in a sheep-pelt rider's coat,
went down to the barn under a half moon, rigged the
blood bay and left the yard in a dead walk heading for
Tandy Meadow by way of the cattle trail she had
thought Marshal Holt would have used.

Of course he probably had left the trail, gone into
dense forest somewhere along the trail. He was
running for his life. She already knew how wily he
could be.

She could not have explained to herself why she
was making this ride. There were already four men
hunting Everett Holt. They would not need help,
particularly from a woman.

It turned cold, predictably, the scimitar moon
glowed above an eerie world of silence and space.
The blood bay had been through this country many
times years back, but he remembered. He also walked
with his head up and moving. He had no more desire
to meet carnivores who ate horseflesh than did his
rider.

Some kind of foraging critter was surprised at her
arrival and went smashing through roadside brush
and timber. The blood bay horse tensed with her as
though he would shy, but she patted his neck as the
blundering rush diminished. He came up on his bit
and hiked along as before, except that from here on
he tested for scents, listened for sounds and watched
for movement.

She was better than half way to the meadow when a
man appeared without a sound. The horse hauled
back in a snorting stop.

It was the man she knew as Ben Tuttle. He seemed as surprised to see her as she was to see him. He said, 'This ain't no place for you, ma'm.'

'Why isn't it, Ben? It's my land.'

'What're you doin' riding up here in the dark?'

That remark brought colour to her face, which was now invisible. 'I couldn't sleep. I was curious about the marshal … Mister Hyde is up here with you and John Lane?'

'Yes'm.'

'Did you know a man riding with the marshal called Jeff?'

'Yes indeed. I caught him an' a younger feller an' left them tied to some trees.'

'Mister Hyde shot him dead when his arms and legs were tied. Shot him through the chest with me standing there.'

The rangeman's reaction was not a surprise. 'Miz' Scott, he told us what the marshal an' Jeff done. Burnt his house down with his family inside it.'

She frowned. 'According to Jeff when we talked before he was killed, neither he nor his nephew were in the country. He said the marshal burned those people by himself.'

The rangeman shifted stance, hung both thumbs in the front of his shellbelt and looked steadily up at her for a long moment before speaking again. 'I expect it wasn't anythin' a man would want to remember he'd had a hand in. But Hyde's story says Jeff rode over with the marshal, folks saw them ridin' toward the Hyde place in the night.' The rangeman paused before also saying, 'Maybe it's one of them things no one'll know the truth about. Jeff's dead an' we got Marshal Holt dug in on the west side of the meadow in some trees where the underbrush is thicker'n the hair on a dog's back.'

'Why are you down here so far away, Ben?'

'Just in case … Mister Holt's as sneaky as a coyote an' as slippery as a snake. We run him up that slope and never seen him again, but he's up there. The four of us got plumb around where we can see him leave that brush patch no matter what direction he goes.'

Evelyn knew every yard of the territory the rangeman had described. Along with her knowledge about Marshal Holt's cleverness and the dozens of hidden game trails where they had last seen him, she would not have wagered a busted cartwheel Marshal Holt wasn't already a long way off and still riding.

Her rider guessed her thoughts and shook his head. 'He's up there, ma'm. A gopher couldn't get past the four of us.'

She shrugged. In the dark, a man like Everett Holt who was struggling desperately for his life. …She said, 'Ben, I know you'll leave the country now … I'd like you to answer a question for me. It's personal and I know I shouldn't ask but we've been friends a long time ….'

'I killed him, Miz Scott. Shot him off the high seat of the stagecoach. I had to. He had already got off a couple of shots at me. It was self-defence, except that I hadn't no right to stop the stage in the first place, an' for all I got out of it I'd just as well have let it roll on by … In the strict sense of the word it wasn't murder. In the eyes of lawmen like Marshal Holt it *was* murder. You're right, as soon as this is over we'll never see each other again … Miz Scott, it'll be up to you to figure whether it was murder or not. But what Holt did was to my figurin' worse than what I did. I know – two wrongs don't make a right … Ma'm please go back. They'll come back to the ranch when it's over. Just don't ride ahead another yard. Hell's goin' to break loose come daylight.'

The outlaw stood briefly looking up at her, then turned and lost himself amid the trees in the darkness where the moonlight did not reach. He was right, they would never meet again.

She dismounted and stood with her horse for a long while. Later, probably much later, she would wrestle with a judgement about what her rangerider had done. Right now there was an impending showdown up ahead on the meadow named after her parents.

TWELVE
The Unexpected

John Lane and Bob Lytle, whose interest in Marshal Holt was grounds for what they were doing, running him to earth if they could, lacked the elements which had kept Max Hyde so zealously on the lawman's trail. It was his idea to split up, cover every trail and every possible pathway out of the meadow.

Hyde was a zealot. Barnes told John Lane with a wag of his head the only thing on this earth that would stop Max Hyde was a bullet. Lane had agreed without saying so.

When cold set in on Tandy Meadow the men hunkered near their tethered horses. They had, as Barnes had told Evelyn Scott, split up and were now waiting for daylight to tighten their surround.

Despite the cold each man on Tandy Meadow had plenty of time for private thoughts. Whatever else they might have excused, deliberately burning a woman and two children to death could never be excused.

John Lane was in the timber on the east side of the meadow. He waited for visibility to improve. His middle had not stopped hurting since he'd met the others in the barn. It was more like an enduring stomachache than pain from a bullet, but regardless of the definition it was still pain. He wanted to smoke but refrained, not because he thought the scent would travel but because the flare of a match even inside his hat would attract instant attention by reflection. The night was totally dark after the moon departed.

He hoped the horse he had ridden had eaten lately because he had no rope to tether it with and no hobbles.

A cougar screamed somewhere in the darkly shadowed south and seemingly also to the west.

Lane smiled to himself. If that didn't discourage the forted up lawman from trying to lead his horse in that direction before mounting up and making a horse race of it, Lane was at a loss what would, although big cats rarely attacked people, particularly armed ones, in isolated country where cougars had practically no contact with men, their attitude was unpredictable.

The horse stood like a stone long after the last echo had died. He was listening for the diminishing echo to cease when both Lane and the nervous horse heard another sound, this time coming from among the trees behind them somewhere.

The horse's attention switched to what he perceived as another possible threat. John Lane rolled flat on the ground facing the dark tangle of trees behind his waiting point.

The sound came and went, stopped and started. If it was a two-legged creature it seemed to stop to listen before starting forward again. It was approaching John Lane's position on a diagonal angle which would pass him some distance farther off among the timber and darkness.

He alternately tried to see what was moving and

looked at his horse whose little ears were up, whose head was high with distended nostrils.

When the horse abruptly lost interest John Lane lowered his head in a resting position with his gun tightly held, right up until whatever was passing back yonder abruptly stopped dead still, and moments later bounded swiftly through the timber going eastward.

Lane blew out a breath and sagged. The fading sound was recognisable; a deer, probably a big buck, had detected man-scent and had fled.

Lane sat up again, put his back to a rough-barked pine tree and resumed his vigil.

His thoughts wandered. Dawn would be along directly. After that the initiative would lie with the cornered federal lawman.

The handsome woman was probably back in her house trying to sleep. By now she would know from Bob Lytle what had happened and which way the fleeing man and his pursuers had gone.

He could not make out the lake because of darkness, but he thought of his time of easy living down there until the woman had arrived like a harbinger of trouble. Beyond that he thought of her in a detached manner.

He wondered about her husband. What kind of a man would settle for a female partner with iron in her backbone?

Evidently the kind of man who liked strong females. She was good-looking, but hell most women were who didn't have too much age on them. Particularly to men who hadn't been around female women in a year or so.

A night bird called. The men who heard it had an identical thought. Not only Indians had mastered the art of bird calls. They had used signals since before whiteskins came over the mountains. Whiteskins had learned from them.

Lane waited for its mate to reply. None did. He might have risked a night bird call to elicit a response from the other bird but he was not that good at it. Some men could imitate birds well enough to deceive other birds. John Lane was not one of them.

He arose and swung his arms. The cold was very noticeable before dawn. He squinted across the meadow, could not even make out the dilapidated log house, sat down and speculated about the man who was buried over there somewhere. And the woman. It came to him that the man had been hard-headed, which was where his daughter had probably got her hard-headedness. He also thought of something else; if she as a young girl had been the only female in the country, and the Scotts' only son had been the only rutting male, it would probably be natural that they would be drawn to one another – warts and all.

He smiled, rubbed his scratchy chin and eyed the horse. It was dozing; cold did not bother it at all.

That night bird called again and this time there was an answer. One bird was northward somewhere, the second one to call was southwesterly.

Lane flexed his hands to keep them supple. One thing he had surmised was that anyone who could draw one of those double-action Colt pistols as fast as he had seen Marshal Holt do this, was probably – in broad daylight anyway – a good shot.

Unless Holt was gone, had got away in the night, there would be a killing to inaugurate the new day. If Hyde didn't kill Holt, then someone else would, but if Holt killed his nemesis, things could become difficult.

Lane was as moderately handy with a sixgun as the average rangeman was, but he was not in the same class as Marshal Holt.

He knew nothing of the ability of Lytle or Barnes with weapons, but surmised they would not be in Everett Holt's class either.

Someone yelled as the darkness first began to fade. It had to be Max Hyde, neither Barnes nor Lane had occasion to force things.

'Everett! Start praying you son of a bitch!'

Lane waited for a retort, thinking taunting the lawman was not necessary. If he hadn't figured out he was surrounded by now, Hyde's yell would convince him of it, while simultaneously alerting him to the position of at least one of the men seeking him.

The silence returned and lingered as daylight increased with agonising slowness. When John Lane could finally see across the meadow as far as the old log house, visibility was only fair. It would improve but not until the sun was higher than the tallest trees on the east side of the meadow.

John Lane sat against his tree waiting for visibility to improve. Barnes was north, Hyde was south, Lane was east. Wherever Holt was holed-up, somewhere in the vicinity of the log house, he could command a good view of the entire meadow.

Someone would have to weasel around over there to find the darned screwt. It would not be John Lane, he was too far across the meadow to make the circuit around to that side by using timber for cover.

Hyde yelled again, but more westerly than before. 'Everett! You had all night to remember their screams and cries. I'm goin' to send you to hell remembering!'

John Lane moved among the trees to his right in order to see up behind the log house. There was no sign of a horse or a man over there. He was beginning to think they had wasted a whole damned night; that Marshal Holt was probably down-country as far as that town Scott ranch got supplies. If this were so, Max Hyde could start all over again, only the next time he would probably never find Marshal Holt.

He was about to go a little farther to the right, which was north, when he saw movement across the meadow where the clearing narrowed and more trees stood not too far from the lake and the Scott ranch trail to and from summer feed.

He hunkered and waited. The movement was furtive. What puzzled him was that it was moving shadowless in the direction of the meadow where there were no trees still standing, near the log house.

Marshal Holt would never be where that shadow was occasionally detectable.

That was Barnes's territory but the stalker over there was not Barnes, it was not tall nor thick enough. Lane did not believe it would be Hyde, not doing what that person was doing. Hyde would never abandon the most likely route out of Tandy Meadow which was south. That was the area Hyde had particularly wanted to stake out; he knew it was the lawman's best route of escape. It led down-country, in every other direction the land was either northward or too rough.

An unexpected event happened over yonder where night-gloom lingered among the trees; a second stalker appeared, this one heavier and taller.

John Lane recognised that second person instantly. It was Arthur Barnes. He was clearly stalking the first person Lane had seen weaving among the trees.

Lane tried to match the illusive first stalker with Bob Lytle, the man they had left at the ranch, but Lytle, while not much taller, was thicker through the chest and shoulders.

It was unlikely that Lytle would be up here anyway; unless he had walked and Lane did not consider that at all. Lytle, like every rangeman John Lane had ever known, never walked anywhere, which was why God had made horses.

The first undefinable shadow abruptly became no longer visible. Lane was so engrossed in this affair he temporarily forgot why he was on the meadow. He watched Barnes reach the gloomy place where Lane had last seen the first person. Barnes did not hesitate, daylight would have helped, in darkness disturbed pine and fir needles looked like all the other tinder.

Barnes slipped ahead, slightly crouched but with no weapon in his hand, looking for all the world like a man with a powerful reason for finding the individual who now appeared to have vanished.

Lane wanted to shout, to re-direct Barnes, but he remained silent. Whatever else was going on up here, Lane's total dedication, like that of Max Hyde, was the federal marshal. Barnes could take care of whoever that ghost was, or he could forget the ghost and return his full attention to watching for signs of Marshal Holt, which was the only reason he was up here.

Lane's horse stamped. Impatience seemed to be part of the make-up of some horses. Others were willing to doze for considerable periods of time, usually older animals. Young horses like young people, possessed annoying urges to be doing something, even if it wasn't important.

Lane looked down where his horse was, returned his attention to the spit of timber where Barnes had been trying to catch what he probably thought was an interloper. There was no sign of either of them.

Shortly now a rising sun would crest above the

treetops, flood Tandy Meadow with glass-clear dazzling sunlight, and reveal every moving thing. If Marshal Holt had not got away last night, in broad daylight he could not do it without a lot more luck than John Tandy thought he had.

Max Hyde yelled again, from a different position. 'Come out, Everett.'

This time there was a harsh response. 'Come and get me, you scatterbrained son of a bitch!'

For John Lane that settled whether the marshal had somehow got past the watchers last night. Now, Marshal Holt was available. Lane privately thought Holt yelling back for whatever reason, was very likely going to be his last mistake.

Holt had to know the kill-crazy zealot would be moving in the direction of his voice. Even if he'd had no experience in situations like this, intuition would have warned him. The new day was still chilly and would remain that way for another two or three hours.

Hyde's recklessness broke the deadlock. He yelled as he stalked the lawman behind the cabin. John Lane saw him twice when he was exposed between tall patches of manzanita. He was back by his horse when he saw this and told the horse Max Hyde was acting like a crazy man; he wasn't forcing a fight with a greenhorn, Marshal Holt was as deadly as a coiled sidewinder and a hell of a lot more *coyote*.

A single gunshot sounded up the slope behind the log house. There was no second shot. Lane moved closer to the clearing looking for powder smoke. It was there but where Lane was standing the log ruin blocked his vision.

The silence settled again, deep and lasting. Lane scanned the meadow from both ends, there was no movement and no sound until Hyde yelled again. He had evidently used the quiet time to re-load and creep closer. Lane could not see up behind the log house. He was beginning to move northward when all hell broke loose somewhere up behind the log house where a spit of tall trees and a thick stand of flourishing underbrush existed in a slight fold of the land.

The gunfire seemed to John Lane to last longer than it did. Afterward there were resounding echoes to heighten the impression of an enduring exchange of shots.

This time he moved northward looking for a position where he could see better. The sun was above treetops but there was still a chill in the air; it was still early morning.

Hyde did not yell again. Lane wondered whether his lack of respect for the gunmanship of his adversary had not proven fatal to him.

Now, with silence and cold sunshine, whatever ending that fight had brought about, John Lane thought he and Arthur Barnes should start stalking the area behind the house, which Barnes could do faster than John Lane could, the distance was much shorter for Barnes, who had already been somewhere closer among the thin stand of trees north of the cabin.

His trouble was simply that with no more gunfire, no more wild screaming by Max Hyde, he had no idea who had survived that furious battle, or whether either man had.

He started the long hike southward staying within the first few fringes of trees all the way around. He moved briskly.

Wherever Barnes was, he should arrive over

yonder long before John Lane did. As Lane widened his stride and was coming around the southerly end of Tandy Meadow where trees were fairly thick, he listened for any indication that Arthur Barnes had already found at least one dead man, perhaps two.

He was approaching the log ruin on the west side of the meadow when he heard someone yell and fire a gun. The voice was high with a chilling sound of terror in it. Lane shortened his stride but only for a moment or two, then continued northward until he could see the log house.

He was less than a hundred yards from the house when another of those bone-chilling screams sounded. This one was accompanied by the unmistakable roar of an enraged bear. Lane stopped, stepped to the edge of the timber and looked in the direction of the house.

Molly!

There was no sign of a bear but the noise coming from inside the log house was unmistakably being made by an enraged bear. There was not another scream from the man who had ducked into the cabin, probably to escape his adversary in the draw behind the house.

A man's instinctive and natural reaction to jumping into an old shack and finding a large bear facing him would be to shoot. That may have been what the man had done, if so, since the bear was still tearing the house apart, the man had either missed her completely or had stung her with a wound that aroused her fury.

John Lane went a little closer. He did not see another person emerging from the trees northward and slightly south of the cabin, who stood as still as a tree, clearly as shocked by the roars and other noises as John Lane was.

The enraged bear roared deafeningly, the echoes

riding wind currents for a great distance. Every animal who heard, stopped whatever it was doing to gauge the distance between it and the roaring, and the direction from which the roaring was coming from.

There was not an animal on the continent who could handle an enraged bear. Not even another bear.

John Lane held his sixgun in his right hand as he crept closer. He finally saw movement ahead, north of the cabin and thought it would be Barnes. It wasn't. Lane stopped dead still. Looking across at him from a fair distance was Evelyn Scott.

The noise diminished but did not stop. Bears grumble, whine, caterwaul even when they are walking alone in the timber. This noise was partly a growl and partly a whine.

Evelyn Scott left the trees heading for the cabin. John Lane yelled at her. 'Don't go over there! She's killing mad! She's not your pet now. Give her time.'

The handsome woman's stride lessened until she stopped. She turned slowly and went back into the timber where she faced around.

John Lane found an old deadfall and sat on it. Finally, heat was reaching the high country.

There was no sign of Arthur Barnes. In fact a day later there was still no sign. He was gone.

THIRTEEN
Tandy Meadow

As John Lane sat in warmth listening to the diminishing sounds of the old sow bear, the handsome woman called to him. 'Did you see who went in there?'

He not only hadn't seen who had entered the old cabin, for all his wandering thoughts the previous night it had not once occurred to him that Molly would still be in what she clearly considered her home, her private territory.

'No,' he replied to both questions. 'Get comfortable and wait.'

Evidently she obeyed because she neither appeared nor spoke again.

John Lane leaned to peer up behind the log house in the direction of that overgrown cleft in the westerly slope. There was nothing moving, no noise, not even any birds chattering.

Whoever had opposed Max Hyde up there was either still up there, probably dead, or at least unwilling to try and sneak away, which would have been hard to do in broad daylight.

The bear's anger was ashes by the time John Lane decided to get closer to the cabin. The bear was whining, making her snuffling sounds. He wanted her to leave the cabin but the longer he waited the less likely it seemed that she would do that.

He was only a stone's throw from the doorless front opening when Molly's massive head appeared in the opening. Because the man stood still she did not see him, but she rolled and wrinkled her nose until she caught the scent, then looked in the right direction but still did not make the visual distinction between his motionless silhouette and the backgrounding growth and shadows.

He called quietly. 'Molly.'

There was blood dripping from the old sow's mouth. She did what most bears do during periods of confusion or indecision, she rocked slightly from side to side.

The second call brought a different response. From the opposite side of the cabin standing clear of the backgrounding growth, Evelyn Scott scarcely raised her voice.

'Molly, are you hurt?'

She started walking slowly toward the big sow, who continued to rock slightly from side to side as she watched the woman coming toward her. The woman kept up a continuous conversation, her voice softly crooning.

John Lane cocked the pistol at his side and watched. Blood to a bear, its own blood or the blood of a kill, made an unpredictable carnivore more dangerous than ever.

Molly stopped rocking as Evelyn Scott came closer, blood dripped, her massive head with its little sunk-set eyes watched everything the woman did.

John Lane scarcely breathed. In his opinion the handsome woman was doing something both provocative and suicidal.

There was something John Lane did not know; females of all categories instinctively felt something, perhaps a vague, cloudy kinship with other females.

Molly slowly gathered her massive body. Lane raised the cocked sixgun. Molly rocked back and sat up like a dog – and made a whining sound that almost sounded like she was crying.

The woman did not hesitate. She stopped directly in front of the old sow, leaned and softly brushed the bear's head. John Lane's finger tightened inside the trigger guard.

The woman withdrew her hand, wiped blood on her riding skirt and speaking softly again, used both hands to trace out the source of blood.

The man who had run into the cabin, who had screamed and fired his pistol, should have done better at such close range. Maybe he was aiming at the head, which most bear hunters could have told him was the poorest target not simply because bears have inordinately thick skulls, but also because the skull from the eyes back sloped, bullets commonly ran a rounding course without penetrating the bone.

But this was not what had happened. The man had fired in terror. The slug had entered Molly's mouth, broken two teeth and had exited in the lower cheek. There was bleeding, but the wound itself was not fatal.

Molly whined as the handsome woman used a blue bandanna to wipe blood away so she could look closely at the injury. The sow was probably in less pain than other critters would have been under identical circumstances, nevertheless she finally raised a massive paw with three inch curved talons and brushed the woman's hand away.

John Lane sat back down. Nobody would ever
believe what he had watched the woman do to a
wounded bear.

He holstered the sidearm and walked slowly toward
the cabin. Evelyn spoke from the side of her mouth.

'Stand still and be quiet.'

He obeyed both orders. The sun was hot on his left
side, the meadow sparkled with drying dew, the sky
was flawless, in all directions there were vestiges of
eternity; nothing that mattered had changed in this
place since the beginning. A woman, a man and an
injured bear were trivial objects, temporary
passersby.

Evelyn interrupted his reverie. She talked Molly
into leaving the cabin to go down to the lake with her
where the injury could be properly cleansed. Lane
watched them walking side by side, the handsome
woman with a graceful stride, the old sow bear who
would have waddled when she walked even if she
hadn't been pigeon-toed like most of her kind,
shambling along beside the woman.

Lane was thirsty. If he'd thought about it would
also have been hungry. He went over to the cabin and
leaned in the doorway, but only for seconds.

The man who had run into the cabin would have
been unrecognisable except for his hat, his torn
shellbelt and the one side of his face which was
un-marked. The rest of him was splattered on the
walls. Max Hyde had died a terrible death.

John Lane went back out into the sunshine. He no
longer had any appetite.

He breathed deeply for a few moments then moved
to the north side of the house where he could see up
to that overgrown cleft where the sounds of gunfire
had sounded like a war was in progress.

There was nothing moving up there and no sounds. Across where he had left the horse, birds were singing. Such was the interlude between life and death. The eternal flowing and ebbing of time noted violent events in seconds. What really mattered like distance, that massive crag overlooking the yard of the Scott ranch, a turquoise sky, rocks, even lakes and renewing grass, were indifferent to the tribulations of two-legged creatures whose span of existence was too short to make an impression.

Molly grumbling down by his old camp brought Lane out of his reverie. He went over where he had first seen the handsome woman, seeking sign of Arthur Barnes. In daylight it was fairly simple to track, and back track to the point where Barnes had returned to his horse, mounted up and rode due westerly, around the lake and out through the miles of old-growth timber. He clearly had decided how the confrontation in Tandy Meadow was going to end, and since the conclusion would occur with or without him, and because he had a long way to go, he had gone on his way.

John Lane went down to the lake, but stood back among the trees where his old camp had been to watch the handsome woman and the old sow. They were both content, Molly was no longer whining, the handsome woman was caring for the old bear as though she were a child.

Lane turned back toward the cleft behind the Tandy cabin. He made little effort at concealment. Hell, for two hours he'd been standing out in plain sight.

Now, the sun was almost directly overhead. Wild bees were busy among patches of underbrush. As Lane started up the hill behind the house the bees zig-zagged in menacing annoyance, which he ignored as he kept to cover while he climbed toward the shadowy pines with coarse brush most of the way.

What surprised him, and also answered a question about flourishing growth in the fold of hillsides was a spring of clear, cold water. He drank, mopped off sweat and continued his climb.

His second surprise was when a horse nickered. He recognised that particular sound, but first he had to find the marshal. The horse had been standing all night, so he would be hungry, but with hours of direct sunlight on him he would also be thirsty.

Everett Holt had had several opportunities to sneak away and evidently he hadn't otherwise the horse would not still be up in there.

John Lane finally saw his horse, its head and neck anyway, the rest was hidden by underbrush. He stopped to listen, heard nothing and was ready to believe that the gunfight which had driven Max Hyde down out of here to seek shelter in the cabin, had probably resulted in the lawman's death.

But he moved carefully in his search, taking longer than it would have taken to reach the edge of a clearing where he halted, stood as straight as he could, parted some wiry branches and looked out into a sparsely overgrown place where evidence of an old fire showed among dead bushes and blackened rocks.

Marshal Holt was sitting out there with a gun in his lap listening. He had detected someone's approach. Lane eased down, drew his Colt and spoke without raising his voice.

'Toss the gun away, Mister Holt.'

The marshal recognised the voice. 'Well now,' he said in that unctuously congenial voice John Lane had come to know very well. 'Well now, Mister Lane, it's a relief to know who's been comin' up in here. I figured it might be Max.'

John Lane said it again. 'Throw the gun away.'

The older man made no move to obey. 'Where is Mister Hyde?'

'Dead and as busted up as a gutted snow bird. Did you hear that bear?'

'Yes sir, an' it made my hair stand straight up.'

'The old sow was in that log shack down yonder. Max Hyde run in there after you'n him fought it out.'

'That was it. I figured something had to get that bear mad. A man could have heard her two miles off … she killed Mister Hyde?'

'She tore him loose from end to end. He shot her in the mouth an' she went after him like only a bear can.'

The marshal made a little clucking sound. 'Too bad. I wanted to do that job myself.'

'Marshal, for the last time, pitch that gun away.'

'Mister Lane, I'd do it except that there's them other fellers besides you.'

'They're not up here. One is back at the yard, the other one rode off … his name was Barnes.'

For a moment Marshal Holt was silent, then he said, 'I'll get him. If it takes the rest of my life I'll get him.'

'I told you, Marshal, to get rid of that gun.'

'Or what? You'll shoot me? Mister Lane, there ain't no bullets left in the gun. It's plumb shot out.'

Bees came into the clearing. Marshal Holt swatted at them using the hand not holding the weapon.

John Lane could have believed the marshal's handgun was shot out, he and Max Hyde had shot at each other enough times to have emptied several guns.

'Throw it aside anyway, Marshal.' To emphasise

what he said John Lane cocked the gun in his sweaty fist. There was no way to mistake the implication but Marshal Holt neither moved nor tossed aside the weapon in his lap.

He said, 'Mister Lane, I been shot, can't stand up. I never been this helpless in my life.' The marshal made a fumbling, feeble effort to move the hand holding the gun in his lap. 'Back's busted I think. I can't lift my arm to get shed of the gun. I told you – it's empty anyway.'

John Lane straightened up a little and gently pushed some thornpin branches aside so he could see the older man.

There was blood on the lawman's trouser leg. It could be the result of being shot in the back. It could also be the result of being sliced through the hip.

Holt said, 'Come take it, Mister Lane. Empty gun ain't no good to me even if I could raise it.'

Lane raised up until he could look over the top of the underbrush. They looked at each other over a long moment. Marshal Holt was sweaty-shiny, his colour was bad, he still showed that habitual small smile. 'Done for, partner, can't move m'legs or both my arms. I figured to set here until the buzzards come … Max won't get the privilege of seein' me die. That's some comfort.'

Lane holstered his sixgun after easing the hammer down. He was about to step clear of the underbrush to approach the man with bloody trousers when a voice as cold as ice spoke from somewhere behind the marshal in the shadows of some old pines.

'Stay where you are, Mister Lane!'

Both men were startled. The last time Marshal Holt had seen the handsome woman was in her yard. The last time Lane had seen her she was caring for the wounded bear at the lake.

John Lane searched for her in the shadows behind the wounded lawman, did not see her until she stepped from the lee side of a huge old sugar pine. She had a little nickel-plated revolver in her hand that looked like a toy.

She did not take her eyes off the lawman as she came closer. When she stopped about thirty feet away, slightly behind and on the left side of Everett Holt she said, 'All right, Mister Lane. Get his gun.'

She cocked the little pistol.

The marshal turned his head until he could see her, and smiled sorrowfully. 'Missus Scott, you're talkin' to a dyin man. You don't need that gun.'

Her reply was distinct and curt. 'Marshal, when Mister Lane was coming up through the brush I got here first, behind you.'

Everett Holt nodded acceptance of that before replying. 'I been shot in the back, ma'm, my legs is numb an' I can't use my arms.'

She did not waver. 'I saw you bat at bees with your arms, Marshal.'

He continued to crane around looking at her for a moment, then blew out a long, unsteady breath. John Lane watched the older man try to twist for a better look at the woman, and lunged for the gun, which was a mistake, he knew how deadly the older man was with a weapon.

The shot that downed Lane sent wildlife fleeing in all directions. Lane did not hear the second shot, less loud, more waspish sounding.

Marshal Holt, in the act of swinging the gun from his lap in the direction of the woman, took her bullet between the eyes. At thirty feet or so she could not have missed if she had just aimed the barrel as she would have pointed a finger.

Everett Holt slumped, killed instantly.

The handsome woman stood like a statue for moments, then dropped the little gun, went over where John Lane was lying, rolled him face up, saw how dark the pupils of his eyes were and choked back a groan of anguish. Blood was soaking the shirt under her hand. She tore the shirt loose, used a soggy blue bandanna which was already pink to wipe away blood for a better look at the wound, then bit her lip, stood up, removed John Lane's shirt, made a bandage of sorts around his upper body, went after his tethered horse and could not quite hoist his limp weight over the saddle. Not until she had tried three times, the last time with breath whistling past her teeth.

She had blood over her blouse, arms, hands and skirt. She tied him to the saddle, led the horse carefully back down to the meadow, left it standing there until she had retrieved her own animal, then started down the cattle trail for her yard.

Part of the way she had to support John Lane, but shortly before they reached the yard – with Bob Lytle standing wide-legged watching – the wounded man floated back into a kind of hazy consciousness. He may have recognised the woman, he certainly looked at her right up until he sagged and Bob Lytle helped him to the ground.

They got him over to the main-house, to the bed he had occupied before. Lytle made a clucking sound and wagged his head. He had seen chest wounds before. Few men survived them, never to his knowledge one who had been bleeding like a stuck hog from Tandy Meadow to the yard of the Scott ranch.

Evelyn gave crisp orders, rarely looking up from the unconscious man whose blood was ruining her blankets and sheets.

Bob Lytle obeyed whatever the woman said, efficiently and solemnly. His personal opinion, which he kept to himself, was that the best thing they could do for John Lane was darken the room, leave him quietly to die in peace.

Evelyn Scott was reacting differently. She got the bleeding down to a trickle, but the path Holt's slug had taken was through the lung. That kind of injury commonly caused a lung to collapse. They were over thirty miles from Berksville, but even if they hadn't been, the old army doctor who practised down there could do little for John Lane's kind of injury except fill him with laudanum and go hunt up the local minister.

FOURTEEN
Toward Winter

People didn't believe in miracles, they called them coincidences, or luck, or attributed them to something they knew nothing about, the ability of the human carcass to mend itself, given sufficient time and decent care.

The lung had not collapsed, which *was* a miracle, but it was almost ten days before the handsome woman and her rangeman stood at bedside and exchanged a look.

Lane's breathing was laboured but steady and even-sounding. Because Bob Lytle was a pragmatic individual, and had heard of folks dying from a collapsed lung, he accepted John Lane's good fortune as part of a healthy man's inherent toughness.

Evelyn Scott, being a female, thought otherwise; when it was a man's time to die from a grievous wound, he died. When he did not die it simply was not the time for him to die, whatever the reason.

She was an excellent nurse. At the end of two weeks with John Lane on the mend, and with little else to do but lie with his thoughts, he had an inkling about her tireless solicitation, she watched over him day and night.

She should have had children.

He'd wondered a little about that back on the meadow while watching her care for the wounded bear. Her touch was light, her attitude was caring, her understanding and anxiety seemed boundless.

One evening when she was rustling supper Bob Lytle came in un-announced, sank down on a chair near the bed looking sweaty and dog-tired and spoke without any preamble, which was his way. 'Partner, in my time I've done some jobs that just about ruint my disposition for a while … I gathered up the pieces of Mister Hyde and buried him. Should have done it sooner … I was hungry until I finished. After that I had no appetite at all.'

'How about the marshal?' Lane asked, and got a crooked, pained look from the rangeman. 'He wasn't there.'

They considered one another for a moment. John Lane did not ask if it had been the bear and Bob Lytle did not say whether it had been or not.

Evelyn Scott appeared with a supper tray; she and her rider exchanged a look and a nod. Lytle left to go and clean up at the washrack behind the bunkhouse.

It had been a warm day without a cloud in sight. As the handsome woman arranged the tray for him she said, 'You recover fast, Mister Lane.'

He considered the mounded plate, the pie and crockery mug of black java. 'It's the care a man gets, Missus Scott.'

She accepted the compliment showing pleasure in her expression. She sat on the chair her rider had recently vacated. 'Ben … Barnes is probably out of the territory by now.'

'Yes'm, I expect he is.'

'I wish he could have stayed, Mister Lane. He was as

good a man as we've ever had on the ranch.'

Lane attacked the food, his appetite had steadily increased despite a lack of physical exertion. Dusk was on the way, shadows in the bedroom made the woman and the man look ten years younger.

'Mister Lane?'

'Yes'm.'

'I think you'll be laid up a long time. Into winter and maybe until next spring.'

He chewed, swallowed and avoided looking at her. 'Not if I can help it, ma'm. I'ver already been so much of a burden on you I'm ashamed of myself ... I'll leave before the leaves fall.'

She shook her head. 'It was a very serious wound, Mister Lane.'

He put down the knife and fork and looked straight at her. 'I'd like to ask you a question.'

'I'll answer if I can, Mister Lane.'

'Don't it seem to you we been through more in the past few weeks than some folks go through during their entire lives?'

She did not hesitate. 'Yes, I think that's right.'

'Well then, damn it all, couldn't you call me John instead of Mister Lane?'

She did not bat an eye. 'John.'

He smiled but she did not. He felt colour rising in his face and went back to eating. She broke the awkward moment with a dry remark. 'You'll be here through the winter, so I hope you like to play checkers.'

He wanted to sigh in exasperation, instead he said he'd played his share of checkers, usually when the weather was too bad for men to be outside. What he did not say was that even if winter arrived tomorrow, he would not be here when it came if he had to walk and lead his horse.

The following day Bob Lytle rode out of the yard shortly after daybreak; the usual routines had been neglected during the trouble that had ended in four burials.

With plenty of time to cogitate he considered what the aftermath would be; deputy US marshals did not disappear without someone, somewhere, eventually becoming curious.

When he got back to the ranch shy of sunset he cleaned up before crossing to the main-house to mention this to his employer and John Lane, who were together in the bedroom when Lytle came along.

It was nothing the handsome woman or John Lane had not considered. Lane bluntly said, 'Lie or tell the truth. If we tell the truth you can bet there'll be marshals up here to take us away to be tried, an' whether it amounts to anythin' or not, it's goin' to waste a lot of time.'

Lytle leaned in the doorway. 'Lie,' he said. 'There's just us three who know what happened, an' I got a bad feelin' other federal lawmen wouldn't believe what we know about Marshal Holt, what he done here an' elsewhere.'

Evelyn was faintly frowning when she said, 'Lie?'

John Lane made an attempt to make it easier for her. 'Not exactly lie. We just agree to say that he was here with two friends lookin' for a fugitive who wasn't here.'

Lytle shook his head. 'Remember what Holt said about how he found Barnes? Someone down in Berksville recognised Barnes and sent the marshal up here.'

Lane was gazing at the cowboy when he replied. 'I didn't say he didn't come up here, I said he came lookin' for a fugitive ... He didn't find him because the fugitive wasn't here. If they ever catch Barnes he sure as hell isn't going to tell them what happened ... they'd hang him for being involved.'

Bob Lytle looked pleased in a bleak way. 'Half truth, half lie?'

Lane nodded and put his attention upon the handsome woman. She surprised both men. 'My husband told me one time he had known men he were sure had broken the law. They said nothing he did not ask ... that would fit Barnes wouldn't it? He rode for us four years, was as good a man as we'd ever had on the ranch, and that was all we were concerned with ... So he worked for us that long then saddled up, drew his pay and rode on. And yes, Marshal Holt was here looking for him, and when Barnes was no longer around, Marshal Holt and his friends rode off.'

They had a cup of laced coffee on that, and rehearsed it so well they could be convincing when the time came.

But it never came.

With summer passing, leaves turning, chill winds coming off the top of Castle Crag's eternal snowfields, and Evelyn and her rider heading out each morning to bring cattle down from the highlands to winter near the home place, John Lane practised walking. At first he was as weak as a kitten, but after five days of touring the house his strength returned. The wound had healed some time earlier. The scars would go into the grave with him, but that was unavoidable, and in any case he was glad to be alive with so little to show about how close he had come not to being alive.

He surprised Evelyn one chilly morning by appearing in the kitchen where she was preparing breakfast with the tray in place on the table upon which she put his food before taking his breakfast to him in the bedroom.

She stared from her place by the stove. He smiled. 'Good morning, ma'm.'

She said nothing. He was fully dressed, even to the gunbelt and hat. She reached for a chair and sat down. Eventually she said, 'You're not ready, John. Winter's coming. There's no need for you to leave.'

He wrinkled his nose; something was burning at the stove. She went over there, removed the iron skillet to cool and returned to the table with a cup of coffee for him. It was as hot as original sin so he let the cup stay where he'd placed it as he said, 'My horse's rested long enough, an' I'm ready too. I've been exercising the last week or so. The wound's healed.'

'John ... I'm shy a rider. We've got to start gathering the cattle and bringing them to lower country.'

He'd thought about that too. He probably owed her that much, although except for her nursing him back to health, none of what had happened had been any responsibility of his.

She asked where he would go and he smiled a little when he told her south, that was all, just south until he reached a country where a man's breath didn't freeze in his nose.

She went back to the stove and was quiet so long he did not believe she would say anything more. But she did. 'Bob likes you. He told me few days back you'd fit in and he'll need someone to winter-feed with. And we have to work through to make up a gather for the trail down to the railroad corrals.'

Lane finished breakfast before picking up their discussion. He already knew all her objections, had pondered them for some time. As he pushed the platter away and pulled the cup of black coffee closer, he told her he would stop at that town down yonder and leave word around down there that she needed another man.

Her silence was long again; there was little reason left to doubt that he had made up his mind. She filled her own cup at the stove, sat opposite him at the table and smiled. It was so unexpected he blinked at her.

'I wish you would stay,' she told him.

For two seconds his resolve wavered. The smile'd had something to do with it. She was very attractive when she smiled, the problem was that she very rarely did it. He had an imprint on his heart of a woman who had smiled often. There was very little comparison.

He finished the coffee, arose and dropped his hat atop his head. 'Missus Scott, I'll never forget how you looked after me and all. Someday, if I'm back through this country I'd like to ride in an' visit … Right now, it bein' a little late in the season an' all. …' He held out his hand. She arose as she took it, and squeezed the way a man would have done.

She remained standing at the kitchen table even after the door closed behind him.

At the barn Bob Lytle was currying a pair of horses. He stopped currying, gazed at John Lane with the knowledge forming in his mind that they would probably never meet again.

John got his horse, rigged out in silence, tied his gatherings into place behind the cantle and turned as Lytle said, 'Did you talk to the boss?'

'Yeah … I'd like to stay, Bob, but I've had about all the thirty-below winters I need. For a while anyway.'

'I think she was countin' on you to help through the winter, John.'

Lane sighed. 'I'll leave word down at that town south of here that she needs a hired man. There's sure to be some riders out of work what with winter coming and all.'

'John ...?'

Lytle crossed the distance and held out a thick, work roughened hand. They shook. 'Look after her,' John Lane told the rangeman.

'Yeah, except that she don't need no lookin' after,'

'They all do, Bob, even the ones with a ramrod up their backs.'

Lytle went out front with John Lane, leaned on the tie-rack as Lane swung across leather and said, 'You figure to come back this way someday?'

Lane evened-up his reins as he replied. 'I honestly don't know, Bob. Maybe. But it'll be summer if I do. You take care of yourself.'

'You too.'

The sun was high, the sky was clear, visibility was perfect as Lytle leaned on the tie-rack watching John Lane head for the Tandy Meadow cattle trail. He was back currying the horses when Evelyn arrived, booted and spurred to ride. She was bundled inside a Hudson's Bay blanket coat with pelt-lined gloves in the pocket. She saw which way her rider was gazing and turned. John Lane was already becoming indistinct as he passed by stands of timber.

Her expression was set. She said nothing as they both entered the barn for their saddle animals. Her old dog, who had missed everything, was stretched out in a sunny place on the porch.

She led the horse out front, turned it once and swung into the saddle. She looked southward as her rider was mounting and said, 'They're hard to find, Bob.'

He saw which way she was looking and curtly agreed. 'Yes they are.'

'Did you know his wife died last year.'

Lytle was pulling on his gloves as he replied, 'I figured it had to be something. He wasn't a drifter.'

They left the yard riding slowly northeasterly where they had seen cattle the previous day. John Lane was riding in the opposite direction when a little cold wind whipped up. He was protected from it until he came out of the timber with the broad expanse of Tandy Meadow dead ahead.

He watched the lake for jumping trout, saw none because this late in the summer there were no May flies to attract them, hunched deeper into his coat when the wind hit him, and started on an angle southwesterly across the meadow. He avoided looking at the cabin, but after passing it he turned.

Molly was over in front of the log house watching him. On the spur of the moment and for no particular reason he tied his horse to a tree and hiked back toward the log house.

Molly watched without moving until he called her name, then she sat back on her big behind like a dog and whined her recognition.

The man stopped a fair distance away; it was impossible not to respect anything that large and terrifying. He talked to her for a moment, until she looked southward in the direction of the lake, which made him laugh.

'No fish, old girl. You got to wait until someone else comes along … Molly, take care of yourself.'

She watched him walking back where he had left the horse, and whined. Maybe it meant something, maybe it didn't, bears were chronic whiners, but as he reined on his way he waved back at her.

The wind picked up even after he was in big timber again, its force blunted but not its chill. He saw shod-horse marks and followed them as far as a broad game trail. They kept heading west where he turned south.

By now Arthur Barnes was a hundred miles on his way and most likely still going. Killing a man was somewhat like getting too close to a skunk, the aroma remained in a man's nose long after he had encountered the skunk; a killing would last even longer in a man's mind.

When Lane was crossing a clearing on the downhill trail he had a brief glimpse of open country below which seemed to stretch forever. It was ideal cattle country, at least during the riding season, but this was cold country anywhere a man went.

He did not see the town of Berksville until the following day about mid-morning. It looked like a dozen other cow-country towns he had seen, with a very wide main roadway, stores on both sides, a church steeple with an askew cross atop it, and wind-scourged hardpan roads.

He aimed for the stageroad leading into Berksville from the northeast. He would visit the saloon and the livery barn, two places where riders out of work commonly left their names and where they could be contacted.

He would buy a bait of feed for his horse, maybe sleep up off the ground until the following morning, then start riding again – south. Always south until he came to country where when the autumn sun shone it had actual warmth in it, which was not the case in the north where the sun might shine as bright as new money and while a man was out in it his breath steamed like smoke.

It was six years later while sitting on the porch of a hotel in cow-country northern Arizona that he found a dog-eared newspaper long out of date, and read it while waiting to go to supper across the road at the cafe when he saw an article that brought everything back to him in a rush. The article said the well-to-do-widow of Henry Scott of northeastern Oregon, had gotten married to a man named Robert Lytle, and that they were honeymooning in Arizona, over at Phoenix.